Three Flings

Doris

Jean

In all thy ways acknowledge Him,

and He shall direct thy paths.

Proverbs 3: 6

Shadows in the Fog

"Miss Amanda, come away from that window." Emma straightened the crocheted coverlet on the brass bed and gave each feather pillow a thump.

Amanda held open the curtain of her seventh-floor hotel room window. Along the narrow tree-lined street below, hotels crowded the sidewalk and soared above the steep ravines. In their midst, like an oasis among their plaster columns and wrought iron balustrades, a small untouched plot of green lawn ran back to the mountain where a narrow stream trickled down to form a shallow pool. Amanda could just make out a tall form, dressed in black, dark hair curling around his collar, standing by the pool. For days she had watched him from the window.

Every morning, he materialized out of the fog to fill his jug at the hot spring. He sat straight and tall on the bench by the pool, yet his shoulders drooped when he walked away. Something about the man, maybe his air of tragic loneliness, filled her imagination until she found herself weaving daydreams about him. *He is tall and kind with a smile that lights up when he sees her. His thick hair twines around her*

Steam rose and mingled with the cool spring air, creating a fog that danced about the pool. The nook in the far corner of the lawn looked like a pair of hands folded then re-opened just enough to invite others to share its secrets. The spa had built a retaining wall round the pool but hadn't ruined the natural beauty of the recessed cove, hidden at street level but visible, even in the fog, from her upper story window. Every morning, the fog seeped across the manicured expanse of the lawn, then rose like a lifting veil when the sun heated the air. The man by the pool moved as though part of the fog and Amanda longed for the chance to match reality to imagination.

"You must get ready now." Emma emerged from the dressing room and held out a white linen gown to Amanda.

"I don't want to go, Emma. I'm not sick. I'm not old. I don't need their treatments." Amanda let the curtain fall; so much for her view of the outside world. She seemed to spend her life looking at the world through gauze curtains. The light coming through the sheer fabric reflected off the flowered wallpaper making the whole room seem blue and hazy. The gloom suited Amanda's mood.

Her parents sent her to this spa in the mountains to cure what they termed her 'nervous disorder.' Never in her twenty-one years had she felt so helpless. Amanda assumed all the attention a certain suitor had been paying her necessitated her sojourn at this spa. After all, Hiram lacked 'financial stability' and a man without means simply did not exist in her father's world.

"Oh Emma, I would love to drive one of those new automobiles or ride in a flying machine." She let the nightgown fall from her shoulders.

"Miss Amanda, whatever gives you such ideas?"

"I want excitement in my life." Amanda sat on the edge of the bed. "I want to do things, go places. Can you understand that?"

"I understand, Miss Amanda. When you are married, you can do things. In the meantime, your parents think you need to be here. Now, come." Emma brushed Amanda's hair and pulled it into a chignon then helped her into the loose-fitting gown Amanda wore for her treatments.

"I'll go, but I'm not sick." Amanda turned the brass doorknob; the cold metal, shined daily by the maids, made her think of the man at the pool. His uniform had brass buttons. Did he have someone to shine them for him? Or did he have to polish them himself? Did she dare go talk to him?

"You don't have to go, Emma. You can finish hemming my

dress."

"But your father…" Emma said, her hands clenching in her apron.

"Oh, Emma, father is not here. And anyway, lots of girls are wearing their skirts in a far more risqué manner." Amanda said, pulling the door closed behind her before Emma could object.

Once in the hall, Amanda ran down the stairs, her slipper-clad feet making no sound on the thick Turkish carpet. She let herself out the side door and ran across the lawn to where the waterfall cascaded down the side of the mountain and emptied into the glistening pool in the nook. The full sun never touched the pool's quiet depths, and only the whispering of the wind and the distant trickle of the water coming down from the mountaintop to the valley below disturbed the stillness.

But she was too late to see him face to face. His back was turned as he walked, toward the rising sun, outlined in golden light. She had watched him from the window so many mornings but never dared try to speak to him for fear Emma would cable her father. Tomorrow, she would just have to find some way to escape Emma's watchful eye. She must stop letting fear of her father determine her actions.

Back inside, she made her way to the treatment chamber. The Grand Hotel's high, white ceilings reflected cold blue light from the electric sconces lining the hall. Thick brocade draperies hung over windows at the end of the halls and burgundy flocked wallpaper from Paris extended floor to ceiling. Paintings in gilt frames lined the hall, glowing in the artificial light. Of course, her father would send her to the most exclusive place.

The Hot Springs Grand Hotel more than lived up to its name, with its tall, white columns sweeping up seven stories of the façade and still more stories above those until the entire structure blotted out the sun. In the afternoon, elderly couples lounged in white wooden rocking chairs along the porch running the length of the Italianate building. Ladies with parasols and gentlemen in high hats strolled along the promenade at the foot of the hill. She first visited here on the eve of her thirteenth birthday when her mother needed a rest before the social season began. Amanda had been fascinated with the machine that cleaned the coins; that seemed a lifetime ago.

****

The next morning Amanda rose early, determined to see the stranger face to face. When Emma brought her morning tea, Amanda managed to knock the cup over, spilling hot liquid across the Persian carpet._Emma stooped to clean up the mess._Amanda insisted she fetch another cup first. She waited just long enough for Emma to disappear down the servant's corridor, then slipped down the stairs and, easing

the side door closed behind her, ran outside. He was there, by the edge

of the pool, his back to her. As he leaned over to fill his glass jug, she

<u>stole</u> across the lawn, dew soaking her slippers.

She didn't even realize she had touched his arm until he

jumped. He stared up at her, shaking his head as though uncertain of

what he saw.

"I didn't mean to startle you," Amanda said, taking a step back.

She'd only wanted to make certain she hadn't dreamed him into

existence.

"Are you real?" He reached up as if to touch her cheek but let

his hand fall without touching her. Disappointment stabbed through

her, startling in its intensity.

"Of course, I am real." Amanda spun around so he could see her

from all sides. "I have been watching you from my window up there

and I had to see your face for myself."

He stood up, towering above her just as she had known he

would. He was lean and in the dim light his face appeared sunken.

"Let me see your face." She reached up to touch his cheek, but

he grabbed her hand and held it in his own shoulder as fear of being

found out gripped her 'Had the curtains in her room moved? Had

Emma returned?' She placed his hand against her cheek, held it a moment, then ran toward the side door.

****

Iaon caught his breath. *Was she real?* He'd had no time to call after her. His fingers still held the warmth from her cheek HAs she disappeared into the hotel, he hoisted his jug of water and headed. She kept looking over her

toward the railroad station.

For some time now he had longed for someone to share his world; had his desire created an apparition? An apparition dressed in layers of white gossamer as light as the fog, her blonde hair loose on her shoulders; and when she'd spun around, she'd seemed to be dancing on air, like some woodland nymph. The muscles in his face were stiff as he smiled. Maybe the first smile since he had traveled west to recuperate from The War to End All Wars.

Not that life before the war had been easy in the coal-mining town where he grew up. His father had already acquired the rattling cough that meant a coalminer's death was just around the corner. When the war offered a chance to get out, Iaon had chosen the suddenness of a bullet over the slow certainty of coal dust.

After the war, he landed a job with the railroad. The hard work had strengthened his body, healing his wounds and helping him put his experiences in France behind him. Little by little, he advanced to her the position of Conductor; but the work hadn't been enough to fill the emptiness in his soul. Until today, Iaon hadn't known how the emptiness could ever be filled. With the closeness of the girl and her trembling hand in his, he began to hope his wish had been fulfilled.

****

At the heavy wooden door to the hotel, Amanda turned. Her footsteps left a glistening trail in the dew, but the fog had swallowed the stranger by the pool only the vision of him lingered in her heart. Her damp slippers marred the polished shine of the marble floor as she made her way to the treatment chamber. Might as well get her therapy over with so she could tell Emma she'd gone, if questioned. As soon as she pulled the curtain around the cubicle, she heard Emma asking the nurse about her. Apparently satisfied with the answer, Emma departed. Amanda sighed as the nurse prepared her for the treatment.

****

"The treatments must be doing you good." Emma laid her sewing down and rose to her feet when Amanda returned to the room. "You look much brighter today."

Amanda crossed to the window without answering and pulled

the curtains aside. Sunlight danced off the water and streamed across the grass in the nook below. A warm glow enfolded her now just as nearness his hand cradled in hers.

Amanda let the curtain fall and dropped into the chair near the window. "Emma, do you ever dream of getting away?"

Emma folded away her sewing and smoothed the front of her starched white apron without meeting Amanda's eyes. "I am most thankful that your father took me in when my parents died."

Amanda was quite sure her father's reason for taking in Emma, a ward of the state, had more to do with social climbing than a desire to help. He wished to curry favor with the elite who sponsored the Orphan Project, and hear his name mentioned in the most notable of circles.

"In a few months I will be of legal age," Emma said. "I want to go back to Boston and find my brother and sister."

"Oh, Emma, I didn't realize you were separated from your family." How like her father not to care about the individual, only the appearance his charity created. People thought he was a kind and benevolent man. Amanda knew better. But at least Emma would soon be free to do as she chose. Amanda doubted she herself would ever be free from her father. On impulse, she ran across the room and threw her arms around Emma, holding her close for a moment. But stiff and unyielding, Emma soon turned away.

Sorry for her impulsive action, Amanda returned to the window as the shadows of evening crept across the nook. She had never had a real beau. Her father required money and position in a son-in-law and so far, no one had measured up. Amanda took the curtain in her hand, pulling it away from the window. The fabric is lighter--but maybe it was her mood that had changed. She spun around just as she had done this morning. The hint of gold laced through the blue wallpaper cast a golden glow across the room. For the first time in a while, Amanda smiled.

****

Amanda arose even earlier the next morning sneaking from her room before Emma made her appearance. The dense fog swirled around her, so thick she had to feel her way to the pool. He was not there. Amanda sat on the stone wall, her heart sinking. What if he never returned? Footsteps, echoing off the mountain, reverberating in her heart, stopped her breath. She turned just as he materialized from the fog, his face lighting up when he saw her.

She ran to him and took his hand in hers, holding it against her face. His touch was light even though the hand she held was rough. He stepped closer. His heart beat against her arm. Warmth radiated from his hand down to her heart, setting it aflame.

Brown eyes, the color of darkest coffee, looked deep into hers. A red puckered scar marred his face--a brand from a fire so hot it melted the skin. Amanda's heart skipped a beat. The burn ran across his cheek, down his neck, and disappeared beneath his hairline. She reached up to touch his face but he grabbed her hand, pain flickering in his eyes. Amanda could only imagine the humiliation of being stared at, pitied by those who looked out of curiosity. She reached to touch the scar and heal his inner agony.

"Your name?" she whispered.

"Iaon."

"Iaon." The strange name rolled off her tongue. A crunching sound of gravel from the walkway behind them made her turn. She dropped his hand and ran toward the hotel.

****

Iaon reached for her, but she slipped from his grasp.

"And yours?" he called after her.

"Amanda." The answer drifted back as she disappeared into the fog.

The wind responded with a soft moan that seemed to come from the very depths of the earth. A sound so sad and mournful that Iaon shivered as he plunged his jug into the pool and then hurried away.

A cannon's backfire had taken the side of his face that day in the Argonne Forest. Iaon could live with that loss. But the incessant stares wore on his nerves. He had lost three comrades that day, and their screams woke him in the night when the wind howled. But Amanda had not run-in disgust at his scar. Had God sent him an angel?

****

Every morning that week, she sneaked out to meet Iaon before he went to work. She learned little of him, only that he worked for the railroad. She told him about her father's domineering ways and her mother's social climbing, but none of it mattered when they sat side by side.

"And what would your father think of me?" Iaon laughed. Amanda could not meet his gaze, she stared at her hands imagining her father's anger if he knew of her friendship with Iaon. She could only shake her head. 'How could she explain her father's ambition to Iaon?'

"My dear," Iaon said. When Iaon took her hand in his, Amanda's fear of her father disappeared.

****

Emma commented on how happy she looked when Amanda returned to the room after her treatment.

"Must be the change in climate," Amanda said, her heartbeat thudding in her ears so loudly that she wanted to cover them for fear Emma could hear. Slowly she spun around and sat down in a chair by the window. She would have to remember to watch her countenance or she would raise Emma's suspicions.

Each morning leaving him hurt a little more. With a song on her lips and a spring in her step, she flew out the side door to meet him. But when he walked toward the rising sun, her heart sank, for then she must wait an entire day before they were together again.

****

The next morning, Iaon was not at the pool. Amanda waited as long as she dared, but he did not come. Her heart ached for him, but she tried to hide her disappointment. She must not let Emma discover her secret. Just a few days ago, Amanda would have given anything to leave the hotel. Now she couldn't bear the thought of never seeing Iaon again.

****

Iaon waited for her at the pool the next day, and she hurried toward him, careless of prying eyes. He clasped both her hands in his strong ones. Was there a tear in his eye?

"My grandmother died. I must go back east."

"But you will come back, won't you?" Amanda tightened her hands around his, fear choking her.

"She left me her home. I must take care of the details."

"But--"

"I must go," he said, pulling his hands free. He turned to go but stopped and pulled her so hard against him that Amanda could barely breathe.

He kissed the top of her head, and Amanda clung to him, her heart pounding against his. He breathed her name but before she could say anything, a whistle sounded from the distant railway station and Iaon released her. She reached her hand out, her fingers grasping the rough wool of his uniform, and Iaon groaned as he pulled her close again.

This time, when he released her, Amanda did not try to stop him and he rushed away from her. At the corner of the lawn, he turned. "Wait for me. I shall return soon."

Amanda slowly made her way to the hotel. He had hugged her. He wanted her to wait for him. A smile crossed her lips. She wanted to shout her joy to the world.

****

Amanda went to the pool every day after that, but he did not come. She sat on the bench every morning as long as she dared, listening to the quiet rush of the waterfall, keeping one eye peeled for Emma, willing Iaon to appear. A week crawled by and still he did not come. Every day, she dragged herself back to the hotel and up the stairs to the treatment room. She never imagined the heartache of missing Iaon could have such an effect on her.

****

On the eighth day after Iaon's departure, Amanda struggled to make it out of bed. She was late. *What if she had missed him?* But Iaon was not by the pool. Her heart sank.

"Amanda."

The fog was so thick she couldn't tell if she imagined the sound.

"Amanda."

It was Iaon's voice. He was coming. She ran to his shadow in the fog.

He wrapped his arms around her and she leaned against him, his heartbeat drumming under her ear.

"Amanda," he said, pulling away from her. "I must tell you about my family. My background is so different from yours--"

"I don't care about that," Amanda said, clasping his hands and pulling him down onto the bench beside her.

"Your father will care. You see, my father worked in the mines," he said, his expression so bleak that Amanda's heart skipped a beat. "He could not find any other work when he came here from Wales."

"Is that how he met your mother?" Iaon turned his face from her at the question.

"Her friend's grandfather owned the mine," Iaon said. "She came for a visit and fell in love with my father. But her father didn't think a coalminer good enough for his daughter. When she married him anyway, her father disowned her. She died when I was only ten." Iaon stared off into space. "I think something in my father died as well."

"I am so sorry." Amanda shivered at the thought of a young Iaon growing up without a mother.

"The war offered me a chance to get away," Iaon said. "I volunteered but I never imagined what the trenches would be like. No one could imagine…" His voice trailed off and he raised a hand as if to touch his scar, but Amanda grabbed his fingers in hers and cradled them to her cheek.

"My grandmother never lost sight of us as the years passed. She would send money," Iaon said, after a moment. "Mother kept it hidden in a small box. Father found it after her death. He used the money to pay for her funeral."

A sob rose in her throat as she threw her arms around Iaon. Tears trickled down her cheeks to wet the front of his jacket. How long they sat entwined, Amanda did not know. The sun came up and the fog began to disappear, and still, they did not move.

****

Amanda could not sleep that night. At dawn, she stood at the window, waiting, her fingers running up and down the sheer draperies. He was there. She rushed out to him, no longer caring if Emma saw her or not. Iaon picked her up gently and swung her around.

"So right," she whispered.

He kissed the top of her head and when he released her and stepped back, he was bathed in the warm glow of the sun.

"My parents sent me here pretending they thought I was sick," Amanda said, drowning in the depths of his dark eyes. "Now, I know I was sick." Amanda placed her hand over her fluttering heart "Sick for love and someone to care about me. But the doctors at the hotel don't have a treatment for that. My cure is right here."

He pulled her close. Her heart slowed to beat in rhythm with his. She slid her hand around his neck, wanting his lips on hers but Iaon stepped backwards, his expression tortured.

"I must go," Amanda said, her cheeks turning red ~~flushing~~ at his rebuff. 'He would not let her get close to him and she did not understand.' She turned, but he caught her hand in his, and pressed his lips to the palm. The imprint seared her skin as a symbol of hope for their future She closed her fist to hold it tight. That kiss would have to get her through the hours until she could see him again.

****

"Where have you been?" Emma met her at the door of the treatment room. "No, never mind. Your parents telegraphed they are coming on the early train and we are to meet them."

Stunned, Amanda allowed Emma to steer her back to the suite. "You must eat your breakfast while I finish packing," Emma directed.

Amanda dropped into a chair in front of a tray of food. She knew Emma had telegraphed her parents she was improving but she had thought there would be more time before she had to face them. Her parents were going west to Denver on some new venture her father wished to investigate. Her mother had hinted in her last letter the venture involved Amanda--that there was someone he wanted her to meet. Would her father really make her part of a bargain to seal a business deal? Amanda knew the answer as soon as she formed the question.

If only she had more time with Iaon. If only she were strong enough to stand up to her father. But it was too late to think of what might have been.

"Hurry now. We don't want to be late." Emma put their satchels outside the door. "You haven't eaten."

Emma's scrutiny scorched her and Amanda lowered her eyes to prevent any trace of her feelings from showing.

"Well, we can eat on the train." Emma held a wrap for Amanda. There was nothing to do but obey. As Amanda pulled on her gloves, she realized she still had her fist clenched. When she opened her hand, Iaon's kiss would be gone. Amanda's knees shook as she left the hotel.

Emma helped Amanda into the carriage, tucking the blanket around her, swaddling her--Father's faithful proxy. Suffocated, Amanda kicked the blanket off. What would Iaon think when she didn't meet him at the pool tomorrow?

The trip to the train station went too quickly. Only moments after leaving the hotel, Amanda found herself on a bench by the front door, surrounded by their baggage, while Emma looked for a porter.

The sun warmed her face and cleared the fog from her mind, but there were only a few until the westbound train arrived. The eastbound train was already loading. People hurried across the platform, carrying satchels and shouting to each other. The noise of the trains made thought impossible and steam clouded her vision. It was all too much. Heat crawled through her veins, leaving her lightheaded and dizzy unable to run, unable to stay and fight.

"All aboard. All aboard for St. Louis and points east," the conductor called.

The bustle and shouting around the opposite train increased. Emma returned with the porter and tried to speak to her, but the din swallowed her words.

"Emma, please get me a drink of water." Amanda leaned her head against the wall and closed her eyes.

"Amanda."

The soft, low call was like the wind brushing her cheek. She turned toward the sound.

"Amanda, what are you doing here?" Iaon stood beside her. Amanda jumped to her feet, longing to throw herself into his arms, but worried Emma would return.

"I must leave today," she said,

Iaon paled and took a step backward as if she had knocked the wind out of him. "What do you mean? Why are you leaving?

"My parents are coming on the westbound train. They want to take me to Colorado with them." She grasped Iaon's hand, unable to resist touching him again. "I don't want to leave you but I am not strong enough to go against my father's wishes."

"Amanda, I have been offered a position back east at the main office. I was going to tell you tomorrow. Come with me now," Iaon begged. "We have only known each other for a month but that is long enough for me to know I love you. Will you come with me?"

The long whistling wail of a train approaching the station, cut across his voice.

Iaon pulled out his watch. "That is the westbound train." He snapped the watch shut. The ground rumbled beneath their feet, shaking her to her core.

He leaned forward, clasping her hands in his. "Come with me, Amanda. I can't offer you the life you have now but we can live comfortably."

"Iaon, I don't want the life I have now. I hate the phony people, the way my mother pushes me to be friends with all the wealthy girls, my father's endless ambitions." His earnest, dark eyes seared into her heart, shaking her as much as the approaching train. She knew what she must do. She would never be able to face her father and beg for a blessing he would never give. But Iaon wanted her and she wanted him. That was all that mattered. She threw her arms around his neck and held him close. His arms stole around her. "Take me with you, Iaon. Please take me away, now."

"All aboard." The conductor's call jerked them out of their reverie.

"My satchels," she said, pointing to the rose-colored bags beside her.

Iaon gathered the satchels and threw them on the eastbound train. Amanda ran toward him. He lifted her onto the train as easily as he had the bags. Then he swung up beside her.

"Miss Amanda, what are you doing? That is not our train. Miss Amanda!" Emma ran beside the track, waving her arms as the train moved out of the station.

"I must go with him, Emma," Amanda called over the noise of the train. "You will be all right. Go back to your family."

Iaon pulled her into his arms as the station receded into the distance. Her heart slowed to beat in rhythm with his. She inched her arms around his neck.-He leaned forward and took possession of her lips. She was his and he was hers.

"I am yours as long as we both shall live," Amanda whispered when she could breathe again.

The westbound train passed, almost close enough to touch. A man stood astride the back platform, smoke encircling his head. The familiar scent of his cigar made her heart jump.

"Such a disgusting display." She could almost hear the words as her father gestured toward the couple embracing on the back of the passing train.

She smiled. There was no hint of recognition from her father, no acknowledgement or good-bye to her family. No, she was no longer the same.

With Iaon's arms around her, she headed east toward the rising sun.

****

Libby's Luck

'All is not right,' Libby thought., 'Derek does not understand.'

She pushed herself to sitting. 'I needed to get up and go to the

bathroom and I needed a moment alone to think about last night. Some

would call it a whirlwind courtship. It had been a whirlwind courtship

and a simple ceremony in his family's living room. They were right in

that assumption. I had no family so what did it matter? I could tell his

family had been surprised at the suddenness of Derek's actions. Didn't

Derek notice the gapping mouths and the piercing stares?" A tear

trickled down her cheek, she wiped it away with the back of her hand.

No use dwelling on the past.'

She pushed up from the sink only to grab it again as the night

before rushed through her mind. She stood at the edge of the group.

Troy, Derek's brother called. Libby put her hand on his chest as he

moved off. 'Why do I only feel safe near him?' Blinking her eyes, she

moved to a wing chair near the dining room. She sat, trying not to cry

and fighting the queasy feeling in the pit of her stomach.

I have no family and his seemed surprised at the suddenness of

Derek's actions. They acted as if I'm someone to be feared. *Is the age difference a big thing?'* She flipped off the light and stood in the darkness. "Why am I talking to a mirror? Maybe it's the way Derek's family looks at me with questions in their eyes sending an uneasy feeling down my spine.

The longing for kindness reared its ugly head. Libby raised her hand to her throat and swallowed hard to force it back down. She hadn't been this scared since she a teenager on her own.

"Am I really beautiful?" Libby asked the reflection in the mirror.1

It was early, the darkness still clung to the earth and the first rays of dawn were still slumbering. Libby thought about returning to bed but knew if she did, Derek would want to make love to her again, and at this moment, she didn't feel so loving. Again, she looked at her reflection. *Does he want kids?* Derek's house was a small two bedroom; one had been his mother's. There was a small front porch and a screened in back porch. The house was just the right size for the two of them, but could it hold three? 2

Scenes from the night before, Derek had been in such a hurry he had popped the buttons on her blouse. He had not been as gentle as usual. He was on top of her, holding himself up with arms so his weight did not crush her. Her mind was not ready but her body responded to Derek's touch. When he entered her, Libby gasped. He began to drive deeper and harder, his motions coming so quick and fast that Libby could not catch up. Spent, Derek rolled over and pulled her close.

"I'm sorry Libby. I should have waited for you. It won't happen again. Please forgive me, Libby. His breathing that just moments ago had been so heavy now was soft and gentle as it blew against her cheek. They lay side by side for the longest time until Derek reached up to turn off the light. Libby pulled the blanket up to her chin and stared into the darkness. She yearned for more, but didn't know what.

Libby pulled on her robe and crept out the front door, being sure not to make a sound. The thought of taking off down the road and not coming back whispered to her from the recesses of her soul. She made it to the gate just as dawn woke up and greeted her by tingeing the dark clouds a light shade of pink. Thunder clapped and rumbled. A storm was blowing in. Big drops pounded Libby as she ran to the porch, shaking herself like an old dog trying to disperse any stray droplet. Still the sun rimmed the earth as rain pelted the ground, as if the two couldn't make up their minds what kind of day it would be. The house sat on a small hill. From the porch she could see the old bridge and the swirl of water that raced underneath. It would not take much rain to send water over the roadway.

Libby retraced her steps. *Might as well start breakfast.*3She could hear Derek up and about. Coffee dripping and sausage sizzling in the pan, Libby bent to put the biscuits in the oven. Derek wrapped his arms about her as she came up. She could feel him against her. He wanted her-again. Derek nuzzled her neck and chill bumps ran down her legs all the way to her toes.

"Nasty day outside," Libby said pushing away to turn the sausage.

He'd brought her home to a nice little house with a green lawn and roses in the corner of the yard. Someone had spent a great deal of time caring for it and now that it was spring, she would love to get outside and enjoy it. A huge oak shaded the side of the house. Libby felt alone and hungered for something she couldn't name.

Rain pummeled the roof. Derek had said that it flooded along the river but he had built his house high enough up so they would not have to worry. The dog tried to get the door open. Libby left the safety of the doorway and raced across the porch to open it. Swollen with rainwater, it did not open easily. The old dog, heavy with pups, shook herself and made for the old basket she used as a bed. Once, twice, three times the dog circled the basket unable to get comfortable.

"What's wrong girl?" Libby came closer. Then she saw it, a tiny head sticking out and with one push, the little creature emerged and landed on the bed. The old dog crawled in with the pup. Libby was delighted. She did not move as she watched the wonder of birth.

How she wished that Derek was there to share it with her. Maybe then she could tell him what she had tried to say for a while now. Maybe he had seen a birth so many times before that he took it for granted. Thunder shook the house once more, bringing Libby back from her reverie.

The day drug slowly. Libby listened to the weather report on the radio; the storm had filled the streams to capacity. Libby did not know if owning a radio constituted a blessing or a curse. Libby walked the floors, always ending at the porch where she checked on the old dog. It had only been her and her father, a never do well farmer. Her mother could not stand the hardship and left when Libby was ten. She had packed her bag and left while Libby was at school. There had been no good-by or any attempt to take Libby with her. Her father had thrown things around and then made Libby do the chores around the house as if her mother had never left. She couldn't keep up and had dropped out of school. That only made matters worse because then she had to put up with her father all of the time. It was a relief when he kicked her out for being lazy. *If her own family had not wanted her, why should Derek's?*

Libby wiped the tears on her sleeve. Four tiny blobs now whined from

the depths of the basket. She sat on her heels and peered down at the

miracle she had witnessed. "Good job ole' girl," she whispered. The

dog blinked as if she understood.

The room darkened. She gripped the arms of the chair as she

listened to the weather report. The river was up and the bridge was out.

She had not been this scared since she had been a teenager on her own.

Libby did not know if owning a radio was a blessing or a curse. She

began to rock back and forth as memories of times with Derek washed

over her. Derek had come to the diner on a rainy day much like today.

He stayed and drank cup after cup of coffee. When Derek asked her to

go to the ice cream social, Libby jumped at the chance. She could see

him throwing a baseball at the milk jugs and knocking them over. He

gave her the cupid doll he'd won. After that, Derek stopped by every

night after work and walked her home. One day he leaned against the

door post and asked, "Beautiful, will you marry me?" Without

hesitation, Libby agreed. They were married the next Saturday by the

Justice of the Peace down the road. Maybe they should have waited.5

The old rocking chair moaned and creaked in rhythm to her

thoughts, scenes of mishap to Derek crowded6 out by the rhythm of the chair. What if something happened to him? She pushed away thoughts of falling logs, and crashing trees. In this rain, he could even miss the bridge. Who knew what disaster might occur? Further and further back she went until her legs were in the air. Only then did she slow the pace until the outside sounds became clear and the incessant tick of the clock droned in her head. The rain stopped and the sky began to clear. Her thoughts tumbled over each other, but none could hold her attention as she concentrated on the door, willing it to open.

The sound of the old Ford sputtering down the road thundered in her head. Maybe his family thought she had married Sal for his money. He was rich enough to own a motorized vehicle. Derek pulled into the drive, and set every inch of her body on alert. She heard the engine die and the tired slam of the door as it shut. Feet scraped across the walk, she heard something drop, and then the scrape of the key as it found its mark. The door swung inward. The moon provided the backdrop to silhouette him. He was massive and easily filled the door frame with his presence. As he stooped to pick up his lunch kit, she pounced, wrapped her legs around his waist and dug her nails into his back. His beard stubble scratched the soft inside of her arms and yet she held on. He swung her round and round until her hair came down from its customary tight chignon and wrapped about her shoulders.

"Troy has always wanted Mom's old brass bed." Derek said.

"That will give us room for the baby. Do you feel okay?"

Libby nodded as she took Derek's hand and lead him to the

rocking chair his father had made. He sat down and Libby curled up

in his lap. She would tell him about the puppies later.

Now she was happy just knowing that Derek loved her and he wanted

a baby- their baby.

****

Olivia

A gust of March wind caught the door as Olivia struggled to pull it shut. The wind grew stronger, as she made her way down the main street. Thunder rolled across the sky and lightning followed in big jagged streaks. The overhead cover ran out and Olivia felt the rain running down her neck. At five o'clock exactly, Mrs. Watameyer had closed the accounts book and headed upstairs to her apartment. Olivia could see a steady drizzle outside but she slipped on her coat and tied the scarf tight around her head. There had been no offer for her to stay longer. The storm seemed friendlier than her boss.

"Well, there is no use standing here in the rain thinking about what might have been," Olivia muttered. The road was already a river. She stepped into a hole and felt the water seep into her shoes and soak the hem of her dress.

Another gust blew stronger and Olivia struggled to move forward, afraid if she fell that there would be no energy to get up and she would lie there in the street until death came to claim her. At times like this, life seemed to hardly be worth the effort. The alternative was slow starvation. Olivia trudged on across the street and up on to the sidewalk. A diner loomed ahead. Seeking shelter under the eaves, she must have leaned against the door, for it came open. There she stood, rain blowing in, running off her coat and pooling at her feet.

"Shut the door," someone yelled. Olivia could not see as the water dripping from her hair ran down her face. She did sense a movement and the sound of the door being shut.

"Sorry, Miss." The voice ushered her toward the counter with a hand on her elbow.

As her vision cleared, she saw a long counter running across one side of the room; there an old man wiped it off. "Might as well sit a spell until this blows over," someone spoke from behind her.
"Miss, you can hang your coat on the rack by the door," the man behind the counter said.

Olivia slipped it off as water ran down and formed a puddle on the floor. She began to shiver; her wet clothes clung to her. The man behind her took the coat and hung it up for her.

"Charlie, bring the lady a cup of coffee."
The man behind the counter turned to the stove and returned with a cup. Olivia could see the steam rising from it. She looked from the cup to the man called Charlie, who seemed to be as round as he was tall. A shock of red hair stood straight up in front and he held a cigar with his

teeth as he worked. Olivia wanted to laugh at the comical sight.

"Thanks so much, but I can't afford this." Olivia clung to her purse as if it could help her find the words to tell about the scarcity of money and that this would be a luxury for her.

"The coffee is on me," the other man replied. "Sit."
Olivia was not use to being ordered about, but she did as she was told. With her hands wrapped around the cup, she sipped the hot liquid that warmed all the way down. She shivered again.

"You have an old sweater back there that the lady can throw on?" the man sat down at the end of the counter.

"Looks more like a drowned rat than a lady," Charlie shot back. "How about letting her use your coat?"

"I left my coat in the truck."

"Convenient, don't you think?"

"Didn't know a lady was going to blow in and that she might have need of it. Now, do you have something or not?" the man leaned over the counter.

"Keep your shirt on there, Sal," he said between clinched teeth. "Don't think so, but let's have a look see," Charlie hunkered down and began pulling things from under the counter and throwing them to the man.

"Charlie, this won't even cover the top of her head." Sal held up a dishtowel.

"Well, what do you expect?" Charlie sat back on his heels. "I have an apron."

"An apron? You can't wrap her up in your smelly old apron," he laughed.

"Let me think now," Charlie took the cigar out of his mouth. "It seems like Millie brought an old tablecloth to cut up for rags. It'll do."

Olivia leaned over the counter. She could not remember the last time anyone made a fuss over her. Charlie emerged from under the counter and handed a bundle to Sal.

"That will do." He shook the cloth out, folded it in half and draped it over Olivia's shoulders. She pulled it tight around her, glad for the warmth.

As the man returned to his stool, she took note of him. He moved with grace for a man over six-feet tall. Olivia felt like a small child next to him. Clean-shaven and the tan revealed he worked outside. He smiled at her, then turned his attention back to his own coffee and the conversation he was having with Charlie.

"If this weather doesn't break soon, we won't be able to get into the woods until spring." He set his cup down and motioned for Charlie to fill it again. "By the way, I'm Salvador Sabbatini, Sal to my friends and the guy behind the counter is Charlie Keegan." Sal grinned and pointed; he had dark hair and brown eyes that twinkled when he smiled.

"I'm Olivia McKay." It had been a long time since she had used her given name.

"Nice to meet you Olivia," Sal reached his hand out then pulled it back.

"Don't you work at the millinery shop?" Charlie asked.

"Yes." Olivia took a sip of coffee so she would not be expected to talk.

"I thought I saw you there when I picked up a hat for my wife," Charlie smiled at her. "You do good work."

"Thanks," Olivia managed to smile at him. She did not remember him, but then Mrs. Watameyer waited on the customers.

"Sorry to hear about your mother, Sal." Charlie picked up the rag and swiped it across the spotless counter.

"She went quickly. Been kind of lonesome around the old place, but work has kept me busy." Sal sat and stared at his cup for a minute. Charlie reached for the coffee pot.

"Want something to eat, Sal?" Charlie refilled the cup and moved toward Olivia.

She shook her head. Charlie put the pot back on the stove.

"No thanks, Charlie," Sal turned to Olivia. "Would you like something?" Olivia shook her head again.

"Doesn't talk much, does she?" Charlie winked at Sal. Olivia kept looking down.

Rain pelted the window and thunder seemed to shake the diner to its very core. One wave of lightning chased another across the sky. Talking ceased as the storm made its self-known. Olivia and Sal sat and drank their coffee. Charlie poured himself a cup. The three sat in silence, turning every now and then to check the windows for any sign that the storm would let up. Nightfall came and the storm continued to rage.

"It must be close to closing time for you, Charlie," Sal set his cup down and pushed it across the counter. "Wife expecting you home about now?"

"Can't send you folks off in a storm like this," Charlie motioned to the window.

"Besides, she is just a wee slip of a girl and the wind would be tossing her about like a rag doll," Charlie said in his best Irish brogue. He studied the girl for a moment. Much too thin for his taste and the mousy hair plastered to her head by the rain made her look homely more than anything else.

"You live nearby?" Sal turned to Olivia as he dug some change out of his pocket and placed it on the counter.

"Over on Bradbury Road," Olivia supplied. She pushed her cup across the counter and slid off the stool.

"That's quite a piece to go in this weather," Sal stood up. "Could I give you a ride home?"

"Thanks, but you don't have to do that," Olivia studied the floor.

"I know I don't have to do it," Sal looked down at the top of her head.

"It will be fine, Miss," Charlie added. "Sal here is all right." Olivia began to fold the tablecloth when Charlie told her to take it.

"You may need it." Charlie busied himself with rinsing the cups and turning off lights. Olivia stuck the cloth under her arm.
She looked from one to the other before she moved toward the door to get her coat, hoping to make a quick exit. Sal already stood there, holding her coat out for her. She slid her arms into the sleeve.

"Wait until I get the truck door open before you come out."
The rain settled down to a steady drizzle. Olivia waited until Sal opened the door before she rushed out. He waited until she seated

herself before closing the door and going around to the other side.

****

Olivia noted the skill with which Sal put the truck in gear and backed up. Buildings were a gray blur masked by the rain and the growing darkness. By the time they reached Bradbury Lane, the rain had started in earnest again. Olivia found it hard to believe her luck that someone she had just met gave her a ride and she did not have to walk home in this. She sat back against the seat and almost relaxed. Sal pulled up in front of the rooming house where Olivia resided for the past five years. Just as she reached for the door handle, lightning flashed overhead and thunder boomed so close that Olivia screamed and covered her ears. Sal reached out and touched her shoulder. She turned toward him and he moved his hand. Olivia could still feel the warmth on her shoulder where his hand had lain.

"I am in no hurry," Sal said. "Why not sit here for a few minutes until the storm lets up a little?"

"You have done so much for me already; I'd hate to delay you any longer." Olivia turned to look at him. He looked her in the eye for a moment.

"Unlike Charlie, I have no one waiting for me at home." His voice sounded so sad. He gripped the steering wheel with both hands and stared straight ahead.

She studied him for a moment. For a big man, his touch had been gentle. The flannel shirt he wore smelled of pine trees. The look in his eyes matched his voice. Thick hair curled around his collar. They sat in silence as the storm moved over them.

After a while, Sal broke the silence, "Do you like your job?" "It's work and I am so glad to have a job," Olivia answered. Once again thinking if she did not work, she would not eat.

"That's not what I asked." For a long moment he looked at her; she squirmed under his constant gaze.

"When did your mother die?" Olivia changed the subject.

"Been three months now. You would have liked her. She worked hard and loved to laugh. I miss her laughter. Ever since Dad died, she looked after the family. Not that the family needed much looking after. They are all grown," Sal laughed. "Here I am doing all the talking."

"That's fine with me," Olivia said. "I like to hear you talk." His voice sounded soft and deep, like talking into a cistern; it made her tingle inside.

"The rain has let up," Olivia opened the door before he could get around. "Thanks."

She jumped out of the truck and ran up the walk before he could object. Once inside, she leaned against the door. When she heard the noise of the truck starting up and Sal shifting the gears, she ventured a peek. He looked back toward the house. Olivia dropped the curtain and ran upstairs.

Her room contained a single bed against the wall and a washbasin under the window. Several hooks on the wall held her few clothes. She hung up her coat and set her shoes by the door. The tablecloth she put under the mattress for safekeeping. Olivia took the pins out of her hair and began to dry it with a towel. She touched her shoulder where Sal's hand rested. A flash of lightning lit up the room, turning it a warm gold for a moment. A clap of thunder sent her scurrying to bed where she pulled the quilt over her head. Sleep did not come. She tossed and turned most of the night, whether from cold or excitement at her impulsiveness, she could not tell.

Olivia had to drag herself up for work the next day and blamed the storm for keeping her awake. She found it hard to believe it was only Tuesday. She splashed water on her face and pulled on the clothes she wore yesterday. They felt damp and her shoes dripped water just like they had when she'd pulled them off. With a quick twist of her wrists, she gathered her hair into a low bun at the base of her neck. No heat warmed the rooms but Mrs. Barlow served a big breakfast. Olivia would slip a biscuit in her pocket and eat that for lunch.

Today, the other boarders lingered over their meal, not wanting to face the weather outside. Olivia ran back upstairs and pulled on her coat. It felt heavy, just like her heart. Some days she wondered why she got up at all.

****

Mud splashed on her skirt as she trudged the mile to the shop. Water ran down the street and the overhangs offered little protection. Olivia put the open sign in the door, noting the front room seemed small and cramped to her today. Display cases took up the space on each side of the door. A mirror on the wall and a chair in front of a small dressing table offered the required fitting space for a hat or a new lace collar. Mrs. Watameyer came down the stairs in another black outfit; this one contained ruffle from the neck to the hemline. There must be a closet full of clothes upstairs as Mrs. Watameyer's waistline expanded each year to the point she would now make two of Olivia. She sat down at one end of the table from Olivia. Neither spoke.

The room suited Olivia fine with its small space and dark interior. Olivia's own world alternated between black and gray with an occasional brown thrown in. The only color came from the feathers, ribbons and fine nettings that lined the shelves. These bright colors decorated the hats that Olivia created. Her employer wore black ever since she put her husband in the ground some ten years past. Mrs. Watameyer was a woman of few words and that suited Olivia fine, having learned the hard way to keep her mouth shut and not speak; silence could make one invisible.

Rain kept the customers from the millinery shop for a second day. The gloom outside extended to the small interior where Olivia sat. Today, the room seemed smaller. The shelves containing materials to make the hats and bags that Olivia labored over each day seemed to close in on her. She did not mind the tedious work; she pulled the lamp closer to dispel the darkness. Mrs. Watameyer worked on the books at a nearby desk. Silence took up most of the day.

Olivia picked up the hat and continued to shape it in her hands. She sneezed and forgot to cover her mouth. Mrs. Watameyer jumped up. "Don't bring your cold in here on me." Before Olivia could say a thing, Mrs. Watameyer ascended the stairs. Before long, the sound of a stove banging and the kettle whistling let Olivia know that Mrs. Watameyer was making herself a cup of tea, thinking it would keep any cold from taking her as it had her husband. A cup of tea would have been nice but no offering came. Olivia held her hands up to the lamp.

The heat soon penetrated her fingers. By noon, she'd finished the hat and picked up the lace Mrs. Watameyer dropped in her hasty departure.

Lunch came and went with the smell of stew wafting down the stairs. Olivia poured some water from the pitcher and sipped it. Thoughts of last night and the warm coffee brought a smile. At five till five, Mrs. Watameyer descended the stairs. She took the ledger book and climbed back upstairs. Olivia cleared her workspace, putting the few scrapes in her purse. She hung the closed sign and braced for the blast as she opened the door. A face appeared in the doorway. Olivia let go of the door and stepped back in panic. She'd seen that face often in the past. The door banged against the wall and Mrs. Watameyer hollered. Olivia grabbed the door and pulled it, closing it from the outside.

****

Olivia did not see the truck. She was trying to decide if she had truly seen a face in the door or just imagined it. The rain fell in a steady stream and she adjusted her scarf around her head. A feeling came over her; she sensed his presence more than actually seeing him. Sal stood beside her on the sidewalk.

"Could I give you a ride home, Miss Olivia?"

His presence sent chills up and down Olivia's spine. Before she could answer, Sal ran to the side of the truck and opened the door. Olivia looked down the street at the rain then back at Sal. She ran to the truck. In a moment he had the truck in gear and headed down the road.

"I hope you don't mind, Miss McKay," Sal looked over at Olivia, "with all this rain, I didn't have to work and I thought of you trudging home in this weather." He turned his gaze back to the road.

"No, I don't mind," Olivia said. She felt a warm glow inside, like the glow the lightning had spread around her room. "Call me Olivia, please."

"Would you have supper with me, Olivia? Charlie makes a good meatloaf."

Olivia looked up at Sal. With only the biscuit for lunch, she felt her stomach lurch. Crackers and a small piece of cheese awaited her in the room.

"Please," Sal caught her eye. "I don't like to eat by myself." "I'll have supper with you," Olivia said. From deep in the recesses of her mind, Olivia shook off the sound of her mother's voice telling her to be cautious. Just this once, she would do what felt right.

"Charlie, two of your specials," Sal called as they entered the diner. He took her coat and hung it on the rack. "Bring us some of that hot coffee as well." He chose a stool at the far end of the counter and

Olivia sat down beside him.

Charlie brought two cups of coffee. He gave Olivia a big smile. "You look drier today, Miss McKay," he winked at her.

"Thanks to Sal," she replied, "call me Olivia, please." She sipped on the coffee. It made her warm inside. Charlie sat two plates down on the counter. Each contained meatloaf and a mound of mashed potatoes. "I can't eat all that."

"Eat what you want," Sal pulled his plate toward him.

"Please," Olivia turned to him, "you take part of this. It is way too much for me."

Sal pulled the other plate across the counter and spooned half the potatoes and meatloaf onto his own plate. Satisfied, he pushed the plate back over to her. She tried to eat measured bites and not wolf the food down. The food smelled so good and her stomach rumbled from hunger; she gobbled the food. When she thought no one looked, she slipped the roll into her pocket.

Olivia sneezed. She turned red, then sneezed again. "We'd better get you home before you catch your death." He paid the bill and held Olivia's coat for her.

This time, after he stopped the truck in front of her residence, he jumped out and opened the door before Olivia could run off. He walked her to the front door, then pulled his hat off and turned it round and round in his hands.

"May I see you again?" Sal looked deep into Olivia's eyes.

"Sure," Olivia could not say no to him after all he had done for her and she knew more than anything else, she needed to spend time with Sal to squelch something that she longed for. Once again, she ignored the gnawing voice that warned her to be cautious.

Sal tipped his hat. Olivia stood, watching him go until he disappeared down the drive. She ran upstairs. As she hung her coat on the hook, something fell out of the pocket: another roll. She didn't think Sal had noticed.

****

Rain started again Wednesday. Olivia sneezed and sneezed as she got out of bed. Knowing Mrs. Watameyer would throw a fit if she showed up sick, Olivia ate her breakfast then went back upstairs to bed. The storm raged outside. She pulled the cover tight and fell back to sleep. Olivia tossed and turned; memories from her past crowded but she pushed them out by thinking of the kindness Sal showed her. Money being as tight as it was, Olivia could not afford to miss work and she worried that Mrs. Watameyer might fire her. She forgot to get a biscuit from the table and at lunch her stomach growled and rumbled in tune with the thunder. She remembered the rolls from the diner and ate both of them. At five, she wondered if Sal had stopped by the shop.

Thursday morning found it still raining. Olivia pulled on her clothes and headed down to breakfast. She felt light after a day of rest. The others came down one at a time. Olivia slipped a biscuit in her pocket; she sat back and enjoyed her meal, knowing that she had lunch. Water ran on the streets. Olivia waded some puddles to get across. Try as she might to hold up her skirt, the hem got wet. Mrs. Watameyer met her at the door. For a moment, Olivia thought she might be denied access.

"About time you showed up," Mrs. Watameyer backed away from Olivia. "Finish up the tatting and start on the lace collars." Olivia breathed a sigh of relief. She hung her coat on a hook in the back. It would be nice to take off her wet shoes but Mrs. Watameyer sat down at the end of the table and started to work. Olivia picked up the tatting and did the same.

By five o'clock, the rain had stopped. Gray clouds hung low and ominous. Olivia pulled on her coat. No truck waited for her at the curb. Olivia stood, looking both ways out the window. No sign of life. A knot formed in her throat. *Silly, you haven't cried since you were a child.* Olivia scolded herself.

She remembered the night her mother died and her father had thrown a lamp at her. He missed; the lamp shattered against the wall. That had been the beginning of his tirades. She shook herself, no need to dwell on the past.

For a moment, Olivia stared at her reflection, so like her mother's: pale skin, long dark hair and eyes the color of the sky. No wonder her father could not stand to have her around as a reminder of his loss. The millinery shop had been a godsend. Olivia did not know what she would have done without it; so few jobs were available to someone with no skills.

She walked home alone, climbed in to bed and let her thoughts turn to Sal. He'd promised her nothing she reminded herself.

****

Friday and payday came. Olivia thought about staying in bed but decided she could not miss two days of work in one week. Patches of blue appeared in the gray sky and water ceased running down the road. She made it to work without getting the hem of her skirt wet. Mrs. Watameyer turned the open sign as she arrived. Olivia went straight to the table and picked up a lace collar. No orders for hats this week meant no scraps of leftover material. Olivia found herself thinking about all the things that had gone wrong. A ray of sun shot through the window and spilled across her lap. *Can't change what happened. Concentrate on the good things.* Olivia could hear her mother lecture. She decided to think good thoughts. Sal had happened this week. Even if she never saw him again, he'd brought her joy for a moment.

At five minutes until five, Mrs. Watameyer placed a few coins on the end of the table. Olivia cleared her workspace and pulled on her coat. On her way out, she swept the coins into her hand and wrapped them in the corner of her handkerchief. The sky contained huge patches of blue. It would be a nice walk. As she passed the diner, she looked in. Charlie busied himself at the far end of the counter but no sign of Sal. She sighed; her heart felt heavy for the first time in a long while.

Olivia trudged up the steps to the boarding house and heard someone call her name. Sal stepped out of the truck and came toward her. She fought the urge to run and throw her arms around him. He smiled up at her from the bottom step.

"Sorry I didn't make it back," Sal began.

"You don't have any reason to be sorry," Olivia told him.

"I could picture you walking to work in the rain and I wanted to be there." He lowered his eyes.

"Sal," she said.

"Anyway, water ran over the bridge and I couldn't get to town," Sal said. "I came around the long way."

"You didn't have to do that," Olivia said, but her heart sang at the thought.

"I know I didn't have to but I wanted to come," Sal said. "Would you go out with me tomorrow?"

"Yes," Olivia clasped her hands over her mouth in pure excitement. After one impulsive act, it became easier to jump at the chance to be with Sal.

"I'll pick you up at ten." Sal headed back to the truck. Olivia danced up the stairs. From her room she could see the truck turn the corner.

She hung up her coat and pulled off her wet shoes. She sat on the edge of her bed and hugged herself. If she thought too much, it would ruin things.

****

Saturday morning, Olivia made her way down to breakfast. She counted out the money for rent. She would have to buy food with the rest. There would be none left for clothes. Her old shoes must last a while longer. Clouds hung around outside but they could not dampen Olivia's mood. She felt like singing.

Most of the boarders still sat around the table as Olivia entered. She sat down next to Mr. Jenkins, an older gentleman who worked at the bank. He read the paper then handed it to Olivia. She gave him her best smile. Upstairs, Olivia folded the paper and placed it inside her shoes to make the soles a little thicker.

At ten on the dot, Sal turned in front of the boarding house. Not wanting any curious stares, Olivia stood waiting and watching inside. She opened the door to the truck as soon as Sal stopped. Careful not to get mud from the running board on her skirt, Olivia jumped in. He looked at her for a moment then shifted into reverse. At the edge of town, he took the road out of town.

"Where are we going?" Olivia looked around confused.

"Don't you think you should have asked that before now?" Sal laughed and the music of that laughter filled the truck.

"Guess I never thought about it," she admitted.

"There's a carnival over in Cedar Rapids. Do you like carnivals?"

"I've never been to a carnival." Olivia felt herself blush. She had done so few things in her life. Sal reached over and touched her hand. Olivia pulled it back.

"To the carnival it is." Sal headed down the street. Olivia sat studying the buildings as they drove past. The ones on the edge of town were one story with a huge façade that made them look like a two story. The gray buildings jammed up next to each other with only an alley every now and then to separate them.

As they came to a street corner closer to town, the next buildings were two stories; most contained shops with the owners living above them. Mrs. Watameyer's shop was here. These buildings had a high front to make them look taller. At the center of town, the buildings were three stories or more. No need for false fronts to make these look taller. Olivia wondered about putting on false fronts and how people hid behind a façade. *Did Sal have a false front?*

Olivia never ventured far out of town. The changing scenery fascinated her. She could feel Sal watching her but she stared out the window. Trees lined the road and fields lay beyond. They passed a farmhouse every now and then. Houses came closer together and the town appeared in the distance. Sal turned into a field. Brightly colored tents lined up, facing each other. People milled up and down the muddy path, headed for the carnival. Sal helped Olivia out. She stood in wonder. Strange noises came to her. She could make out the people shouting but not the animal sounds. Olivia walked close to Sal; all those people made Olivia nervous and excited at the same time.

As they walked down the midway, she looked first right then left. She could not take it all in. They passed booths selling food. Each booth seemed to offer something different: popcorn, hot dogs, candied apples, taffy, and ice cream. Men stood in front of the booths trying to get people to stop. They would yell over the noise of the crowd. At one booth, Olivia saw people toss coins at dishes. It looked easy but the coins did not go in. Sal stopped at another booth. The man gave Sal three balls to throw at milk bottles set up on a shelf. Sal took the ball in his hand and stretched back as far as he could. The ball went sailing through the air and the bottles flew off the shelf. The man behind the counter gave Sal a funny looking doll. The sign read, "Cupid Doll." They ate corn dogs on a stick washed down with a glass of lemonade. A bearded lady stood in front of one tent trying to get people to go in. Olivia shied away from her. The beard made her think of her father.

They passed more booths with prizes lined up against the wall. "Toss a ring on a bottle and win a prize," the sign read. Olivia stood watching a man try his luck. He missed every time. Half-dressed women danced on a stage and yelled at people to come watch the show. One booth had pies lined up in front of people. The gun sounded and the people all began eating. They could not use their hands. One skinny kid finished first. Pie dripped all over his face and onto his shirt but no one seemed to care. All those standing around laughed and patted him on the back to congratulate him on his win.

Kids rode ponies round and round in a circle; Sal led Olivia to a ride that had wooden horses that went up and down and round and round. Lights flashed from a pillar in the center of the ride and music played as the people spun. Sal helped Olivia on a horse. He moved back and sat on a sleigh behind her. Olivia squealed with joy as the music started and the horse began to move. Up, down, and around she went. She did not want it to end. Sal lifted her off and when her feet touched the ground, he held her close for a moment.

"Carousel," Sal told her when she asked about the ride.

A ringing sound drew Olivia's attention. A man hit a small platform with a wooden hammer; a ball ran up and rang a bell at the top of a pole. Olivia looked at Sal. He shook his head. It would be no problem for him to make the bell ring. He handed the man a coin. With one swift movement, Sal swung the hammer over his head and brought it down on the platform. The ball went soaring to the top and rang the bell. Olivia clapped her hands in delight. Sal beamed from ear to ear. The crowd started moving back as a man leading a huge animal with big ears that flopped back and forth and what appeared to be a nose like Olivia had never seen before came around the tent. Olivia reached for

Sal's hand. As they got closer, she stepped behind him. One of the creature's legs looked as big around as Sal. She stared at the creature from around Sal's arm until the pair disappeared. Then she stepped out from behind him.

"What was that?" she said.

"An elephant," he answered. Olivia continued to stare in the direction the elephant had disappeared. "It's getting late and we have a ways to go yet." Olivia dropped his hand, enjoying the warmth left behind. He headed back toward the truck. She took one last look and followed him, holding tight to her cupid doll. The journey passed in silence until he pulled up in front of the boarding house.

"Would you like to go to church with me tomorrow?" Sal twisted his hands around the steering wheel.

"I'm sorry, but I...I can't," Olivia stammered, as she reached for the door handle.

"The rain has stopped and I don't know when I will be able to get to town..."

Olivia slipped out of the truck while he was talking. She could not tell him she had no clothes to wear to church. Better to let it end this way.

****

Sleep did not come that Saturday night. Visions of her father calling her "worthless" and her mother laughing at her for some unknown reason kept crawling through her mind. It had been a long time since her family invaded her thoughts. A ray of sun poked through the curtain and woke Olivia from her restless slumber. She stretched and enjoyed the moment. The warmth of the sun came filling the room and banished the cold to the corners. Olivia washed her face and slipped on her old dress. She would wash the other and hang it up to dry. Her shoes felt damp and the newspaper had dissolved inside.

With a scrap of cloth, Olivia cleaned the mud from the shoes, rubbed in some of the precious leather soap and sat the shoes on the windowsill to dry. Olivia retrieved the tablecloth from under the mattress. Spreading the cloth out, she imagined making a white hat like the girls wore to school. She dismissed the hat idea as impractical. A burn the size of a hot iron glared at her. A shawl to spread over her shoulders could be cut from one side of the tablecloth and undergarments from the other side. The undershirt would be a little short but it would add protection against the chill. Olivia placed her undergarments over the cloth and cut around them.

The shawl barely reached her elbows and had to be held together with a pin. Olivia sat by the window and hemmed the ragged edge of the shawl. She threw it around her shoulders and rummaged through her purse for her grandmother's cameo. She ran her fingers over the surface and moved to the mirror to see how it looked. The sun no longer peeked out from behind a cloud. Olivia pulled the curtain back. The sky showed clear blue and the outside beckoned. Olivia pulled on her shoes and bounced down the stairs. A song hummed around in her head and she wanted to run to the beat.

A familiar noise floated across the yard. She turned toward the street as a blue truck pulled up the drive. Sal jumped out when he saw Olivia. "You couldn't spend the day with me so I decided to spend the afternoon with you." Surprise registered on her face. She was glad to see him.

"Your truck is blue," Olivia gestured to the truck as Sal approached.

"What color did you think it was?" Sal gave his truck the once over.

"Black."

"No. It's blue, just the color of your eyes when the sun shines." He placed his hand under her chin and tilted her head back until he could look her in the eye. He shook his head and released her. "What are you doing out here?"

"The sun beckoned and I gave in. Thought I would go for a walk," Olivia said. "Would you like to join me?"

Sal fell in step beside Olivia. For a while they walked without talking. Then she broke the silence.

"You work in the woods?"

"Yep. I cut the big trees down."

"Isn't that dangerous?"

"If you don't watch what you are doing, I guess it could be." Sal took his hat off and rubbed his head. "I never gave it much thought."

"Exactly what do you do?" Olivia wanted to know more. He put his hat on, and rubbed his chin as if he were thinking.

"I cut the big trees down. Sometimes if the wind is wrong, it can sit down on your saw and you have a problem. Most of the time, the tree falls right where I want it. A new man will get hurt when he doesn't respect the skidder and it runs over him. Logging isn't much different than any other job. You have to know what you are doing and play it safe."

"You play it safe?" Olivia could imagine Sal swinging an ax just like he swung the hammer.

"Of course," Sal laughed. Olivia felt her heart skip a beat.

"Tell me about yourself," Sal broke a twig off a nearby bush.

"Not much to tell. My mother is gone and my father kicked me out," she said it in a matter-of-fact tone. "I work for Mrs. Watameyer five days a week. The weekends are mine to do with as I please."

"Why do you only work five days?"

"That's the way she wants it," Olivia shrugged her shoulders. Silently, she thought that it had to do with money but she kept her thoughts to herself.

"What about your family?" Olivia had heard him mention family.

"My brother Tony and his wife live in town. They have three kids," Sal spoke in the same matter of fact tone that Olivia used. "My sister Marie lives on a farm. They have a couple of kids."

"Do you get along with them?" Olivia studied his face and noted the twitch in his jaw when she asked.

"I go over there for supper on Sundays, sometimes." Olivia changed the subject back to his work. Sal talked about how they selected just the right tree and how to tell which way it would fall. Olivia heard the pride in his voice as he talked. They made the circle and arrived back at the boarding house. The once grand family home was now divided into rooms and Mrs. Bradley took in borders. Olivia could not imagine growing up in a big place like this. It seemed best suited for a hotel but she did like the yard with the shade trees.

"It's getting late and I have to be up early," Sal looked down at Olivia. She sensed he had something to say. "If it is dry enough, we work. I don't know when I can make it back to town." Sal tipped his hat and turned heel. Olivia stood where he left her until the truck disappeared out of sight. A song burst from her lips in a rush of happiness. She sat in a rocker on the front porch, not wanting this day to end. There might have been time to finish sewing the under garments, but just this once Olivia rocked and watched the sunset.

****

Sleep came with dreams of cupid dolls and elephants. Olivia woke to find the sun peeking through the curtain once more. She smiled. The song began humming around in her head. Her shoes felt dry. At breakfast, Olivia managed to sneak a roll. She watched the mud puddles and managed to make it to work without so much as a splash on her freshly washed dress.

Mrs. Watameyer came down the stairs just as Olivia hung out the sign. Olivia pulled out the tatting and started to work. Mrs. Watameyer took up her station where she could look through the curtain and keep a lookout for customers. The hours drug on with not a soul entering the shop all morning. Olivia poured a glass of water and ate her roll for lunch.

That afternoon, Mrs. Gilbert and her daughter came in requesting a rush order on some hats. They were to have tea with the mayor's wife and must have it by tomorrow at lunch. Olivia went right to work. By quitting time, she had one hat finished. Olivia placed the scraps in her purse. She turned the sign and closed the door.

On the sidewalk, she half expected to see Sal's truck. Her heart dropped a little as she shook herself for being silly. Charlie waved at her as she passed the diner. Olivia waved back. A feeling crept up from inside. She kept looking over her shoulder expecting to see someone; who it was, she could not be certain. In her room, she laid the scraps out beside the others. She would soon have enough.

****

Tuesday passed much the same as Monday. Olivia finished the hat for Mrs. Gilbert and put the scraps of felt in her purse. No work waited for Olivia, she sat staring into space, waiting for Mrs. Watameyer to finish with the sale before she broke out the tatting. Olivia studied her employer. Unlike her own bun, Mrs. Watameyer first made two braids that she wound in an intricate pattern around the top of her head. When she went out, Mrs. Watameyer perched a small hat atop her head then pulled a black veil down over her face. It seemed strange to be in mourning for such a long time. As she left, Mrs. Watameyer placed a coin in her hand. Mrs. Gilbert added a little extra for having the hats finished in such short order and Mrs. Watameyer gave it to Olivia. That evening Olivia missed the truck outside. She shook herself to dispel the feelings that surfaced.

After the tea party on Wednesday, Mrs. Watameyer received a couple orders for new hats and several for lace collars and hankies. Social gatherings made ladies compare who wore what and the desire to outdo everyone else came alive. Olivia smiled, happy to be working on hats. She laid the tatting aside and began work on them. Adding color to the drab felt lifted Olivia's spirits. She missed Sal. It was odd, missing someone she had just met.

Thursday came and went with no sign of Sal. Olivia knew that he worked but not seeing him turned out to be harder than she imagined. Payday came. Mrs. Watameyer left the coins on the end of the table. This had been a full week and there would be a penny or two left over. Not enough for shoes but Olivia let the feeling of contentment wash over her.

Saturday came with no word from Sal. Olivia shook herself. Sal made no promises, she reminded herself again. At breakfast, Mr. Jenkins' chair remained vacant, as he had gone to visit his sister. There would be no newspaper to put in her shoes. Olivia finished sewing her undergarments and washed out her dress. She placed the scraps out on the bed. With the smallest of stitches, she would stitch two pieces together; she continued until satisfied with the size. Olivia ran her fingers over the felt to be sure no seam would irritate. She picked up another two scraps and repeated the process. Soon she had two rectangles of identical size. She hid them under her pillow as to such time as she could get some newspaper to complete the job.

At dusk, Olivia found herself on the porch to watch the sunset. She heard a familiar sound. Her heart skipped a beat as Sal pulled up and stopped. He got out of the truck and reached back inside. In his hands he carried a small package wrapped in brown paper and tied with twine. As he handed it to her, their fingers touched. She could feel the electricity that his touch generated.

"It's some material that Mom didn't get made up," Sal said. "I thought you could use it." He extended the package and she grasped it. "Thanks," Olivia said. She wanted to say more but did not know where to start.

"Go to church with me?" Sal said. He stood with one foot on the porch and one foot on a step to be at eye level with Olivia.

"Yes," Olivia whispered. The thought of sitting close to him sent chills running down her spine. She missed him. He made her feel

and that was enough for now.

****

Olivia thought she saw something in his eye. She shook herself.

"Don't read more into it," she told the night air. Olivia held her

package close and rushed up to her room. She undid the string so she

could use it later. The paper would be great for lining her shoes. Inside

were two pieces of material: a blue piece for a skirt and a flowered

piece for a blouse. Late into the night Olivia labored to be ready for

church. The sun woke her. She dressed and made her way to the table.

Mrs. Bradford busied herself clearing the breakfast things. She smiled

as Olivia   came in.

"Sit down," Mrs. Bradford took the dishes to the kitchen and

came back with a cup of coffee and a biscuit. Olivia bit into the biscuit

and discovered a small piece of bacon. She finished the coffee when

she heard Sal's truck in the drive. Olivia met him at the door.

"I will only be a moment," she rushed upstairs for her purse and

her shawl. She finished fastening the cameo as she came down the

stairs. A smile spread across Sal's face. She stopped at eye level.

"Do you like it?"

"You did that last night?" Sal held out his hand and she took it. He helped her down the last two steps. As her feet touched the floor, he spun her around. "You did a great job." Sal kept glancing at her sideways as he opened the truck door for her. She stepped up on the running board and slid in. This feeling of pride swept over her.

"Mom taught me to sew," Olivia said and smiled at the memory. "She could make lace and her stitches were so fine that they did not show."

They slipped into the back seat just as church started. She listened to the unfamiliar words as he sang from the hymnal; his voice washed over her like the rain. As the sermon finished, Sal took her hand and escorted her out a side door. A man went out ahead of them. Olivia hung back. Sal turned toward her with a question in his eyes. Olivia shook her head and the man disappeared. Sal drove to a spot overlooking the river where he parked and helped her out. They walked along the bank, holding hands and talking about the sermon.

"I enjoyed hearing you sing," Olivia told him. Sal grinned. He went to the truck and returned with a basket and a blanket over his arm. He spread the blanket on a fallen log. From the basket he produced a sandwich and handed it to her. He took one out for himself.

"What a nice surprise." She took the sandwich and took a big bite. "This is good."

"I can't take credit for them," he smiled. "Charlie made them. He also sent cake for dessert." Sal set out a jug of water and two cups.

"Next time I see Charlie, I will have to thank him." She took a huge bite of her sandwich and he did the same.

****

The sky turned pink and purple as dusk rushed across the horizon. Sal walked Olivia to the porch of the boarding house. They stood watching the sunset.

"If the weather stays clear, I won't make it back to town until next weekend," Sal paused. "Would you go out with me?"

"It's a long time until Saturday," Olivia leaned back till she could see his face. "If you can't make it you will let me know, won't you?"

"Does that mean you will go with me?" Sal said. Olivia nodded.

"If I can't make it, I will let you know that I had to work," Sal squeezed her hand.

She waited on the porch until she could no longer see the taillights of the truck. Olivia dreaded bedtime but tonight, she was so tired that sleep came as soon as she laid her head on the pillow.

****

"Thought you might like to see the moving picture down at Clarksville," Sal told her the next Saturday as they started off. He focused his attention on the curves in the road. Olivia watched his strong hands grip the steering wheel. He'd changed his flannel shirt for a white one and he wore khakis—both were pressed.

"Yes, I would love the movies." Olivia leaned back against the seat and enjoyed the rhythm of the ride. Soon she fell fast asleep. Sal tapped her on the shoulder.

"We are here." He stepped aside to let her get out.

"I am sorry," she searched for the words. "I haven't been sleeping well at night." Truth be told, she tossed and turned each night; her thoughts vacillating between Sal and her father. She dared not dream but vowed to enjoy each moment with him. What would her mother think   of Sal?

Shoulder to shoulder they watched the movie. Sal took up his seat and overflowed in to Olivia's. She leaned against him; he took her hand. Olivia caught her breath. It was dark inside the theatre and with the movie on there was no need for talking. Just sitting close seemed to satisfy a need in each of them.

The movie ended and Sal stopped the truck in front of the

boarding house.

"May I ask you a question?" Olivia turned in the seat where she could look him in the eye. "Why did you take me home that day when it was raining?"

Sal turned toward her, "Because you had such spunk. There you were soaking wet but you still had an air about you. That and you looked so cute." He laughed and reached out and took her hand. "You make me laugh. I like being around you. I don't want to be alone anymore.   Marry me."

"Marry you?"

"Yes."

"When?"

"Right now," Sal said. "You trusted me before to get you home in one piece. Trust me now to take care of you." He tightened his grip on her hand. Olivia stared at him for a long while. No thoughts rushed through her head. She felt light.

"Yes." He leaned forward and kissed her on the cheek. "You go get your things and tell Mrs. Bradford that you are moving out."
Olivia shook her head up and down in delight. She was getting married. "Do you need any help?"

"No. I can manage," Olivia opened the truck door. "You will be here when I get back?"

"If you like, I can wait on the porch," Sal smiled at her and opened his door.

It just felt more real with Sal walking up the steps with her. Olivia went to her room. She took her old dress down and laid it on the bed. She folded her new clothes and put them on top, then came her few other possessions. The wrapping she saved for her shoes now held her things. With the bundle under her arm, Olivia went to hunt Mrs. Bradford. Olivia found her in the kitchen setting a loaf of bread to rise.

Olivia watched her for a moment; soon she would be doing those things.

"Oh, Olivia dear, I did not see you there." Mrs. Bradford wiped her hands on her apron. "Do you need something?"

"I'm getting married," Olivia blurted out.

Mrs. Bradford let out a whoop of joy. "You marrying that nice man that comes by in the truck?" Olivia nodded. "I am so happy for you, girl."

"I'm getting married this afternoon," Olivia continued. "I just came to pick up my things."

"That is fine dear," Mrs. Bradford grabbed Olivia and gave her a big hug. "Wait just a minute before you go." Mrs. Bradford headed to the front of the house. Olivia stayed rooted to the spot.

"Take this as a wedding present," Mrs. Bradford placed money in her hand.

"I can't take that," Olivia recognized the money she paid for rent just this morning.

"Of course, you can, dear," Mrs. Bradford folded Olivia's fingers over the money.

"If you are in town, stop by and visit me." After another hug, Mrs. Bradford ushered Olivia to the porch. She spotted Sal sitting in the rocker waiting.

"You be good to her," Mrs. Bradford shook her finger at him. "Do you hear me?"

"Yes ma'am," Sal stood and tipped his hat. "I promise I will take good care of her." He took the package from Olivia. Olivia gave Mrs. Bradford a quick hug. Sal had the truck door open. As they drove by the millinery shop, Olivia thought she might as well tell Mrs. Watameyer she would not be in Monday.

"Olivia?" Mrs. Watameyer said as Olivia opened the door.

"I won't be back to work next week," Olivia leaned against Sal for support. "We are getting married." Olivia looked up at Sal. He smiled down at her.

"Very well then," Mrs. Watameyer said. Stooping down under the counter and bringing up a box of gloves, she placed them on the counter. For a moment Olivia thought she might be giving her a wedding gift.

"Olivia doesn't have gloves," Mrs. Watameyer turned to Sal. "Would you like to buy her a pair?"

Sal tipped his hat, turned Olivia around and ushered her out the door without a word. Olivia could hear Sal saying something under his breath but could not make out what. "She doesn't have a hat, how about a hat?" Mrs. Watameyer hollered after them. Sal shut the door.

"We have one more stop." He turned down the street, and she followed. *Where could he need to go?* Sal stopped in front of the jewelry store.

"Oh, no Sal," Olivia protested. "I don't need a ring."

"I know you don't need a ring, but I want you to have one." He pushed the door open. With his hand on her back, he ushered her inside.

"But it's too expensive," Olivia objected.

"I would have bought you one before but I didn't know what size," Sal took her hand and raised it to his lips. With a ring just the right size, Sal and Olivia headed off to the Justice of the Peace. He parked the vehicle in front of a white picket fence. A white trellis hovered over the gate. In the spring it would be full of roses. She stood waiting while he went to the door. Soon they stood in front of the Justice. His wife stood off to the side. She had no family and she had not met his family yet.

Olivia barely heard the words. Sal took her hands in his. "Will you watch over her in sickness and health?"

"I will."

Now it was Olivia's turn. "Do you, Olivia, take this man to love and honor?"

She whispered, "I will."

When he slipped the ring on her finger, she held her hand out to see how it looked. "Till death you do part," the Justice finished. Sal reached in his pocket and pulled out his wallet. Olivia never realized how much money it cost to get married.

Sal beamed from ear to ear as he helped Olivia into the truck. As they rode along, he whistled a happy tune that made her feel warm inside. He pulled up in front of a picket fence.

"Home," he said. He grabbed her bundle and started inside. She stood by the truck. He stopped and watched her look around.

The house, though small, had shutters on the windows. Roses grew in the corner of the yard. Olivia made her way to where Sal stood. He opened the door and stepped back to allow her to step inside. Curtains hung from the windows and a fireplace took up one end of the room.

Sal disappeared down the hall. Olivia continued to explore. The kitchen seemed huge with a nice size sink. A big table occupied half the room. An icebox stood by the back door. She heard scratching on the door and opened it to find a dog sitting on the porch. "See you met the welcoming committee." He wrapped his arms around her. "Her name is Lady."

"Hello, Lady," she greeted the dog. Lady wagged her tail.

"Are you hungry?" Sal gave Olivia a squeeze and headed for the icebox in the corner. He set out a loaf of bread and handed her a knife. She sliced the bread and began opening cabinets, looking for a plate. He disappeared into a small room and returned with cheese and a couple of apples. "Not much of a wedding supper." He placed the cheese on the table and disappeared back in the pantry.

"It's fine." Olivia brought the bread. This time, Sal brought a bottle and two glasses.

He held the chair for her to sit, then poured the dark liquid into the glasses.

"I always keep a little for special occasions." He took his place at the head of the table. "Guess this is as special as it gets." He handed her a glass. She sipped the wine. It burned a little but she liked the warm sensation it gave her insides as it slid down her throat. Sal cut off a big chunk of cheese and began to eat. Olivia took a small chunk. The only place she'd seen a big hunk of cheese had been at the store.

"Eat all you want." Sal motioned to Olivia to take another piece. She took another small one. He ate another huge chunk, then pushed back his plate, drained his glass and scooted his chair back.

"I'll clean up while you go get ready for bed." He pulled her chair out for her.

Olivia went down the hall. She found a bathroom on the right. Her own bathroom; one she did not have to share with boarders. She ran her fingers along the shelf that held Sal's brush and his shaving mug. She could hear him clearing things up in the kitchen. She splashed water on her face. At the end of the hall, the door was closed. She started to open it when she heard Sal behind her.

"Not that one," he said, and Olivia jumped. "That was mom's room."

"This one." He led her into his bedroom: curtains on the windows, a dark rug on the floor and a quilt with lots of green squares covered the bed. He put his hands on her shoulders and she shivered.

He reached up to pull the pins out of her hair. One by one, he pulled the pins out. She shook her head and hair cascaded around her shoulders and down her back. He placed the pins on the dresser.

Sal eased her back until Olivia sat on the edge of the bed. Down on one knee, he removed her shoes and hose. Olivia put her hands on the sides of his face. She could hear his breathing coming in short gasps. Her own heart beat so fast that at any moment it would burst through her dress. Sal placed his hands over hers. He stood up, taking Olivia with him. He began to undo the buttons down the front of her dress. She stood still, not knowing what to do. He sat down in the spot she vacated and as he eased the dress off her shoulders, he kissed the nape of her neck. Chills went down to her very core. He eased the other side off the shoulder and planted a kiss on that side.

The dress fell to the floor. Olivia stepped out of it. When she felt his fingers around her camisole, she raised her arms. Sal pulled the garment over her head, adding it to the pile on the floor. He pulled her close, burying his head between her breasts. The desire to have him rose up in her and she sighed. He kissed her on the stomach. She ran her fingers through his hair. He put a thumb on each side of her underwear, pulled, and the underwear fell to the floor.

"Oh, you are so beautiful," Sal whispered, as he lay her on the bed. She thought she should do something but from where she lay, she could just watch as he unbuttoned his shirt. Black hair stood out on his chest. Olivia wanted to feel it. She leaned up on one arm and ran her fingers down his chest. "Oh, Olivia," he whispered and came to her. She felt the heat of him as he dropped down beside her. Side by side they lay. Sal rubbed her back and whispered in her ear. He moaned and Olivia knew the time had come for her to be his. She gave him the one thing she had: herself.

Sal pulled her over on top of him. Olivia let out a cry when he took the one thing that could never be given back. He was her first. Olivia moved to the rhythm of Sal's body. Her body responded to his as if it had a mind separate from hers. With each thrust, Olivia joined in until Sal let out a sigh. "Olivia, my sweet," Sal whispered over and over in her ear. She curled up close to him. If she moved, Olivia feared she would break the spell. Sal threw the quilt over them.

****

Light streaming through the curtain turned the room a soft green, as if she lay in a field of clover. Sal moved and Olivia moved closer to him. He turned to her, his arm pulling her close. Her fingers tangled in the hairs on his chest, Olivia nibbled at his ear. Sal swatted at her. He kissed the top of her head and made his way down the side of her neck. Olivia responded. She never expected to feel this much excitement, but she had no one to ask about what should be. She would do what felt good. Olivia wondered if her mother experienced such joy as this.

Sal took her again. Together they climbed to the heights and came crashing down the hill together. She lay in his arms: happy and safe.

"Got to get up." Sal rolled over and stood up. Olivia watched as he pulled on his pants. "Come on, Olivia." She smiled up at him. He bent over and kissed the top of her head. "I'll fix breakfast while you get ready to go."

"Go?"

"Today is Sunday and we are having dinner with the family," Sal lowered his voice as if someone listened, "won't they be surprised at what I am bringing." He laughed and the laughter shook the house. Olivia turned pale. She forgot about his family.

She grabbed her bundle and headed for the bathroom. She washed up and put on her new outfit.

"Come and get it," Sal called from the kitchen.

"Just a minute." Olivia drew the brush through her hair and twisted it into a bun. The pins lay on the dresser. She hurried to the bedroom, still holding her hair in a bun. Sal came up behind her and pulled her close. He nibbled on her neck. Olivia felt the shivers run down and the heat began to rise. "If you keep this up, I will never get dressed." She shoved the pins in her hair with extra force. How could she be so silly? She totally forgot his family. What would they think of her? She sat down on the bed to put on her shoes.

"Let me help you." Once again, Sal got down on one knee. He picked up one shoe and held it out. Olivia could see the crumpled paper in the bottom.

"I can do that." Olivia grabbed the shoe. Sal shook his head and stood up.

She pulled on her hose and shoes, and smoothed out her skirt as she went to the kitchen.

He held two plates containing ham, eggs and biscuits; he took his plate to the end of the table. Olivia took a place on the side next to him. Sal moved the plate in front of Olivia. He dug in while she took a mouthful. Sal could cook.

"I'll clear up while you shave and put on a clean shirt." Olivia took the plates to the sink. She heard Sal in the bathroom and shivered. *What do I do now?* Since she had no family, she did not know how she should act around his. He came back, buttoning his shirt, his hair was slicked down and he smelled of tonic water.

"Sal," Olivia turned to him, "how do I act?"

"What?"

"How do I act with your family?" She wrung out the dishrag and hung it over the sink.

"Olivia, be yourself." Sal kissed her on the top of the head and felt her tremble.

He pulled her close and held her until she stopped shaking. "I will be right there. They won't eat you." He tilted her head back and placed a kiss on her lips. A tear rolled out of her eye; he kissed that away. She smiled at him.

Sal stopped the truck under a giant oak. The house was small compared to its neighbors. Sal helped her out and placed her arm inside the curve of his. He led her around to the back of the house.

"Look who's here," a man called. "He's brought company." The man looked like Sal only smaller and whiter.

"My brother, Tony," Sal whispered. Tony came toward them; the rest followed. Everyone talked at once. Olivia held tighter to Sal. They were surrounded and made no progress forward. Sal greeted each one and introduced them to Olivia. The kids became bored and wandered off to play. Sal led Olivia to a table where the grownups assembled.

"Can I talk to you alone?" Tony put his arm on Sal's shoulder. Sal looked at Olivia. He planted a kiss on the top of her head without bending over. Sal was huge but Olivia only felt safe near him.

"I'll be back." He gave her hand a squeeze and followed Tony out of ear shot.

"How long have you known Sal?" Olivia thought the question came from Marie, Sal's sister.

"For a while," Olivia lied and concentrated on her hands. Marie shook her head and joined Tony's wife at the other end of the table. The two put their heads together. Olivia could see them glance her way. She blushed and looked down.

As soon as Sal came back, Marie jumped up and ran to him. Olivia could not hear what she said but she could see the expression on Sal's face change.

"I'm sorry, Olivia," Sal came up behind her and put his hands on Olivia's shoulders.

"We came over today to tell you that Olivia and I were married yesterday." He looked around at the shocked expressions on their faces.

"Come on, Olivia." She stood up.

"That's great," Tony ran forward and began pumping Sal's

hand. "You finally made the leap. Married! I'll be." Marie's husband patted Sal on the back. The women glared at Olivia.

"I have to be to work early in the morning." Sal took Olivia's hand and led her back to the truck. "I am sorry, Olivia." Sal shut the door. Olivia could not keep the tears from rolling down her cheeks. She turned her head toward the window. They rode in silence all the way home.

Sal's family had looked at her with questions in their eyes that made her uneasy. Sal laughed it off. "They'll come around," he assured her. She was not so sure; they had not been rude, but what she would have liked was kindness. Not being rude didn't count, but for the moment she would settle for it. Could she ever find kindness within Sal's family?

"Someone's glad to see me." Olivia bent down and scratched the old dog behind the ear. The dog nuzzled closer to her.

"Olivia," Sal began. "It will just take time." Olivia nodded but deep down she wasn't so sure.

That night, Sal could not have been gentler. He repeated the process of undressing Olivia. First taking down her hair, he stroked the long strands as if to feel each one. Down on his knee, he removed the shoes and hose. Her clothes ended in a pile at her feet, followed by his.

Methodically with slow circular motions, Sal stroked her back and rubbed her arms as if he could take away the ugliness of his family. Olivia relaxed against him; she basked in his attempts to minister to her crushed soul. She pulled him close and felt the heat of his body against hers. Their bodies became one and moved in unison. Sal took her to the heights of love and when she came down, he was there to assure her with his presence.

****

Light streamed through the curtain; Olivia rolled over. She touched the spot where Sal had been and found it cold. She grabbed the sheet and pulled it around her. Down the hall and on to the kitchen, she searched for Sal. Olivia felt the panic rise.

"Morning, beautiful." Sal came in the back door carrying a basket, which he sat on the table. He kissed her on top of the head and turned to the stove. "Do you know how to cook?"

Olivia shook her head and looked at the floor. There had been little opportunity in her life to learn. Sal placed his hand under her chin and raised it. "No time like the present to get started. First, you'd best change." He laughed as the red crept up into Olivia's face.

Olivia remembered the night before and shivered at how cold his family seemed.

She buttoned the last button as she came back into the kitchen. The smell of sausage frying greeted her as Sal hovered over the stove. Olivia peered into the basket and found that it contained eggs.

"You can take care of the chickens and any money you make from the sale of eggs will be yours to do with as you please," Sal cracked two eggs in a pan. "Make a couple of sandwiches while I finish this. We can start cooking lessons tomorrow." Olivia sliced the bread and added thick slice of cheese. Sal pointed to ham that he'd sliced. Olivia added that to the sandwich. Sal pulled out a dinner pail; he added an apple and the sandwiches. He poured coffee into a thermos.

They sat in silence as Sal wolfed down his breakfast and headed out the door. "I won't be home until dark." With a tight squeeze for Olivia and a pat on the head for the old dog, Sal left for work. Olivia stood in the doorway until she could no longer hear the sound of the engine. She returned to the kitchen and began to tidy up; she saved a biscuit and a piece of sausage for lunch.

Time moved in slow motion as Olivia made the bed and swept the floors. She wondered around the house, opening doors and pulling out drawers. Sal had a place for everything and she would learn where things went. A washing machine occupied the back porch but Olivia had no clue how to use it. She washed her dress in the sink and hung it outside on the line. Her shoes could use some paper but Olivia found none. At lunch, Olivia sat on the porch and ate her biscuit. The old dog curled at her feet. The sun warmed her and Olivia, relaxed and comfortable, fell asleep. Thoughts of the night before crept up to haunt her dreams. His family had been surprised at the suddenness of Sal's actions. They acted as if she were someone to be feared. Was the age difference a big thing? Olivia longed to talk to her mother and have the doubts put to rest. She could hear her mother's sarcastic remarks, "You married someone you barely knew. How smart was that! It's no wonder you don't have a clue to how Sal would react."

The sound of the truck coming down the road woke Olivia. She rushed to the gate to meet Sal. He picked her up and swung her around as if she weighed nothing. He went back to the truck and picked up his lunch pail. He put his arm across Olivia's shoulders. "You can put the potatoes on to boil while I clean up." Sal set the lunch pail on the cabinet. Olivia began opening drawers. *Where would you keep potatoes?* He came up behind her and gave her a hug. He pulled on a drawer that tilted out, and inside were potatoes. He took a pot out from under the sink and filled it with water. Sal took one knife and handed one to Olivia, he showed her how to peel the potatoes. Side by side they fixed supper. Olivia knew Sal must be tired but he did not complain.

After the meal, she insisted on clearing the table and cleaning up. He headed down the hall. She heard his boots hit the floor and smiled. Olivia finished the dishes. No sound came from the bedroom but that of his breath being sucked in and let out. She tiptoed to the bedroom. Sal slept stretched out with a smile on his face; she covered him with the quilt. Olivia undressed and curled up as close as she could to Sal. He reached out and pulled her close.

Each day Olivia learned more of the cooking art. Her meatloaf, though not as good as Charlie's, turned out delicious and Sal bragged on it. The washing machine scared her. She caught her sleeve in the wringer the first time she used it by herself. Sal came to her rescue and popped the ringer loose. Olivia wiped the sweat off her face, rolled up her sleeves and continued doing the laundry. He stood back and watched. The smile on his face grew broader. During the week, Sal would be so tired he fell asleep as soon as his head hit the pillow. Olivia would curl up next to him. For a moment, she nestled close to him and relaxed. She took a deep breath to calm her wildly beating heart. She could not believe her luck.

Olivia posted a sign on the gate that she had eggs for sale. One day, a truck stopped out front, and the driver took all the eggs in Olivia's basket. He said he would stop by again. She added the coins to the ones Mrs. Bradford gave her. There would soon be enough for a pair of shoes.

A month passed in a blur of activity. Sal said they would need to start planning a garden. He gave her a seed catalogue. Olivia poured over the pages; there was so much she did not know and Sal, patient as ever, explained things one step at a time.

Sunday morning dawned with a drizzle. Olivia let the curtain fall back over the window. His touch could do such strange things to her body; even when she tried to control it, her body betrayed her. He tilted her head back and took possession of her mouth, his lips drawing her closer and stirring feelings deep inside. Sal led her to the bedroom. He undressed her, and as his hands moved, Olivia discovered that her body responded to Sal's touch in ways she could not understand. For a moment she held back, unsure. He paused, but then took possession of her mouth. His kisses sent shivers up and down her spine. Olivia leaned her head back to gaze into Sal's eyes. The light in them lit up Sal's face. He rolled over and pulled her into the crook of his arm. She could feel his heart beating.

"We are going to Tony's this afternoon," Sal announced at breakfast. Olivia sat upright. She knew arguing would do no good.

Because of the rain, the family had moved the gathering inside. Sal escorted Olivia up the steps.

Marie greeted them with politeness and led the way into the great room. Olivia stood at the edge of the group. Sal brought her a glass of lemonade. As if he sensed how uncomfortable she was, he put his arm around her. "Hey, beautiful." He pulled her close. "Why so sad?"

Olivia wanted to explain but words would not come. The men began to smoke and talk politics. Tony took Sal aside. Olivia saw Sal take something out of his pocket and give it to Tony. He took it and stuffed it in his pocket. She noted the exchange of money.

Left alone, Olivia wandered out in search of a quiet place to sit. To get to the dining room, one must go through the parlor and then on to the kitchen in the back of the house. She found a chair and sat down. Marie did not notice her. She had offered to help earlier but Marie had brushed her aside with, "You're company and company doesn't work."

"She's only after his money," she overheard Marie say as she slammed the over-door shut. "What does Sal see in her anyway?" Olivia flinched at the fierceness of Marie's anger. "She is so much younger than him."

"Have you ever seen anyone so homely?" Vivian spit the words out as if they left a bad taste in her mouth. "Sal married her because she could not find anyone who would have her. He has a blind spot for lost causes."

Olivia put her hand over her mouth as a sob came in to her throat.

When all became quiet in the dining room, Olivia hurried to the bathroom. Was she really homely? She smoothed her hair back into the low bun she always wore. Cool water on her face made her feel better. She could not hide out in the bathroom forever. As she emerged from the door, she bumped into Sal. He looked down at her and pulled her close, she laid her head against his chest.

"It is all right," Sal held her face in his hand. Olivia stayed rooted to the spot.

Sal disappeared and returned with her wrap. He helped her into it. The rain started again as they headed for the truck. Olivia sat in silence, staring out the side window as Sal maneuvered the muddy road. A deluge greeted them as they headed for the porch. Rain ran down her back.

Inside, Sal busied himself with stirring up the embers and building a fire. He took hold of her arms and sat her in a chair. He proceeded to remove her shoes and rub her cold, wet feet. "You get out of those wet clothes," he broke the silence.

Olivia walked to the bathroom and stripped off her wet things. She hung the dress and took the towel to her hair. Sal stood by the door watching. He moved so she could get past him. In the bedroom, Sal pulled back the covers. Olivia crawled in. Sal handed her a cup of tea. Her hands trembled so that she spilled some. Sal shed his wet shirt and crawled in bed beside her. He gathered her up in his arms. Tears brimmed in Olivia's eyes; she refused to let them fall. Her body shook with the effort. Sal held her closer.

She had been lulled into a delicious sense that all was right; but all was not right.

Through the night he cradled her. She felt him stroke her hair and run his hand down her arm. His steady heartbeat coaxed her into a state of peace. His breath on her head reassured her when she woke during the night, yet Olivia slept fitfully. Rays of sun crept across the quilt. A beam touched her face and her hand reached out for Sal but found nothing; she screamed and bolted upright. He soothed her hair and whispered in her ear. She could not make out what he said but she calmed down. "I have to go…" he leaned her back and looked into her eyes. "Will you be OK?" Olivia nodded; words would not come.

She pulled the covers under her chin. Olivia remembered the

night before and shivered at how cold his family acted toward her. She refused to think about the events of the previous day. She closed her eyes tight and sleep at last overcame her.

The smell of coffee woke her. Olivia stretched. The sun tried to break through the dark clouds. She put her hair up and collected her dress from the bathroom. Some cold water on her face and she felt much better. In the hall, the spare bedroom door stood open. Olivia tiptoed down the hall to the kitchen. She found a cup of coffee in her place and sipped it. She heard Sal rummaging around in the spare bedroom, then his footsteps in the hall.

"I'm sorry," he began and sat the shoes on the table. "She doesn't need these now and she would want you to have them." He sat down and pushed the shoes to her. Olivia clasped the shoes to her breast. "I never paid attention." Sal hung his head. She put the shoes on the table and came and stood behind him. She cradled his head and rocked to and fro.

"It's not your fault," she whispered. "I am so used to taking care of myself. I almost have enough money saved."

"You shouldn't need for anything," Sal clasped her arm with his hand. "I'm supposed to take care of you."

"Sal," Olivia stroked his hair just as he had hers last night.

"I will try to do better," he said. "I am new at all this."

"We can learn together," she patted his cheek. "Together."

"Together," Sal said. "What about your father?"

"My father? What about him?" Olivia said.

"You called out to him in your sleep," Sal said.

Olivia's face turned white. She grabbed the back of the chair.

"I need to go to town." He scooted his chair back. "Do you want to go with me?"

She nodded and started around the table to collect her old shoes from behind the stove. Sal grabbed the shoes off the table and handed them to her. She took them.

New shoes with a sole felt so good; she hated wearing them in the rain. Sal noted her stop at the edge of the porch. He swung her up and carried her to the truck. Without putting her down, he opened the door and placed her inside. Olivia settled in. It began to sprinkle harder. Sal stopped the truck in front of the mercantile. "Wait here," he instructed.

Sal headed in the opposite direction. Olivia sat and watched him go. She took this time to ponder the things his family said. Maybe they were right…

As Sal passed the mercantile, she saw Tony emerge and follow him down the sidewalk. He caught up with Sal. He put his arm around Tony just like he did Olivia.

They walked on. Sal stopped and turned toward Tony. She could not hear what they said but Tony headed across the street and then in the opposite direction.

Olivia saw movement out of the corner of her eye. She turned to see a man shuffling down the sidewalk. She tried to stifle the scream as the man who looked like her father turned and stared at her.

It began to rain hard as Sal slid in the seat. "Olivia, what's wrong?" Sal pulled her close. Olivia shook her head. "You will think I am crazy," she sobbed.

"Olivia?" Sal held her tight.

"I thought I saw my father," Olivia said, as the tears streamed down her cheeks. "He threw me out after my mother died." Olivia clung to Sal.

He held her until the sobbing stopped, then put the truck in gear. He did not say anything on the ride home. Olivia glanced at him but decided to wait until he spoke first. Sal reached over and took her hand; still, he did not speak. Olivia found words did not come to her either.

Back at home, he did the outside chores and she made ready for bed. The silence grew. Olivia turned her face to the wall and pretended to be asleep. She felt hurt but could not put her thoughts into words. Sal turned off the light and crawled in beside her. He reached for her and she moved into the shelter of his arm. Sal fell asleep. Olivia pulled the covers closer and drifted off.

He pulled her closer as she wormed her way to the top, panting for air.

"Come here, beautiful," Sal called to her in his sleep. For a moment, she nestled close to him and relaxed. As the drumming in her ears slowed, she matched his movements up and down, it seemed so right. His family thought that she'd married Sal for his money, but that was not true. She had to go to the bathroom and she needed a moment alone to think about what had happened at his brother's house. She felt the nausea sweep up from deep inside.

She had to go. She tugged and pushed against his arm, moving it just enough so she could slip out from under it. With each strike of the clock, Olivia's heart raced. Sal would soon be up to start his long day at the sawmill. She had to have time to think of the best way to tell him.

A quick splash of water on her face and the wave of nausea subsided for the moment. Olivia began to feel better. She ran a comb through her hair and studied the eyes looking back from the mirror were dark and sunk. *Where have I gone?* She thought back over the short time since she had wed Sal. She looked at her reflection. The only time she brought up the subject, Sal had said they would discuss it later. That was the same tone he used when Olivia asked if Sal wanted her to clean out his mother's room.

She felt confused. For a moment, she thought about throwing her arms around him and drowning his face in kisses. What if he rejected her? Olivia knew she was being silly, but...her own father had rejected her, sent her packing. She couldn't withstand that. She would not be that dependent on any man ever again.

****

"Nice day," Olivia said, pushing away to turn the sausage. She could feel Sal behind her; she turned and found him staring at her. "Nice day," Sal said. He couldn't believe how lucky he'd been to find her. He loved just standing near her, drinking in her beauty; but something was not right. Lately, Olivia would almost give in to him then pull away just as she did now.

"Olivia," Sal spoke softly. She turned toward him and his heart skipped a beat. Olivia handed him a mug of coffee. He took the mug and sat down at the table where he could watch her as she worked. She set a plate before him and Sal dug in. "You eating?"

"Sal, will your family ever accept me?"

"We can talk about that later."

Later. That's what he always said.

Olivia began packing his lunch: big hearty sandwiches made with her own homemade bread. At the last moment, she slipped a note in. It said simply, "Love you." She sat the pail next to Sal, poured herself some coffee and leaned back against the cabinet to watch him devour his meal. He pushed himself back from the table and took the pail. As he passed her, he put his hand behind her back and pulled her up against him. For a moment he held her, then kissed the top of her head and headed out the door. She listened for him to leave.

She could hear him shift from reverse to first, and the old Ford threw gravel as he turned out of the driveway on to the road. It was nice to have a paved road and not have to deal with dust like you did on dirt. Sal needed a new truck. Maybe she should have dated him longer and discussed some of these things before they were married. She sat in the chair her husband had just vacated and pinched at a biscuit. She stacked the dishes on the counter and went to the bedroom. She put on her old dress; it was beginning to get too tight around the middle. At the thought of Sal, Olivia wanted him close; she pulled on his flannel shirt. It smelled like him. His shirt smelled of pine trees and the outdoors.

She hugged it closer around her.

She poured the last of the coffee into the mug and made her way to the screened in back porch. The wind picked up and the clouds rolled in. The rocking chair banged into the wall. She ran to the front porch and pulled the chair inside. Back on the porch, she watched the clouds boil up and dash across the sky. They turned black as they rammed into each other. Thunder rocked the sky and sent Olivia inside. Rain came down in white sheets, obscuring the view of the gate and the road. Olivia paced from the front to the back. She jumped as lightning lit up the house and thunder rolled overhead. The yard disappeared under a blanket of water, making Olivia's heart sick. How could Sal get home in this?

The door popped open. Olivia rushed to close it only to be encased in Sal's arms. She wrapped her arms around his neck and kissed him with all the emotion bottled up inside. Sal held her, shutting the door with his foot as he moved inside. Olivia clung to him, not daring to let go lest it be a dream.

Sal backed up to the chair and pulled Olivia into his lap. "I love you," he whispered in her ear as he caressed her with his hands.

"I love you, Sal," Olivia breathed in his ear. "What would I do if anything happened to you?" Lightning flashed and thunder rocked the house. She nestled closer to him. The storm rolled on. He held her. This time she grabbed Sal's hand and led him to the bedroom. She thought she knew bliss, but the joy that shown in Sal's eyes and the eagerness in her own soul surprised her.

Sal's hands began to explore her body. They raced up her stomach and crushed her breasts. He took the tips of her breast and massaged them between his fingers. Olivia felt them rise to answer his unspoken request. She wanted him. The storm raged. Sal rocked her back and forth. Olivia laid her head on his shoulder and drifted off to sleep. Sal covered her with a quilt.

Olivia woke in the darkness. She felt for Sal and his presence comforted her.

She touched his face. He reached up and took her hand in his. She leaned over and kissed him with all the passion she felt building in her today. Sal smiled then a soft laugh came from deep within. "You are a tiger, Olivia." Sal kissed her back and she responded, driving them both onward to the brink. Together they reached the height of desire. Olivia could never have imagined this. Wrapped in each other's arms, they drifted off to sleep.

She became aware of the sun glistening through the window. Sal's side of the bed felt cold to her touch. She grabbed her wrap and headed for the kitchen. He came in the front door.

"Part of the roof blew off." Sal poured a cup of coffee and sat down. "The river rose during the night, so I guess I'll be stuck at home for a few days."

Olivia let out a yelp and landed in Sal's lap.

"I have to get the roof fixed before it rains again," he said, and kissed her. Olivia grabbed his face in her hands.

"I get to have you for more than a few minutes," Olivia said. She jumped up and began to cook the sausage he laid out. "What do you need me to do?"

"Hold the ladder," Sal said.

"Isn't there something more I could do?"

"You don't want the ladder to tip over and me fall off do you?" "I'll hold the ladder," Olivia laughed. "As soon as I put on my old shoes."

Sal held the door open and Olivia danced through. Having him around today made her heart sing for joy. "First, the tree on the roof must go," he said, and led the way around the house. A giant oak lay across the yard fence, its branches implanted on the roof as if it grew there. Sal disappeared and returned with the ax. "Step back."

Olivia stepped to the corner of the yard, still within sight of Sal.

He lifted the ax and brought it down on the tree just like the hammer at the fair. Sal swung and each bite of the ax made a bigger notch in the tree. Soon the trunk separated from the branches and the top tumbled into the yard. Sal backed up just as Lady ran past. Sal tripped and fell over Lady. Lady ran off hollering.

"Sal!" Olivia yelled. She ran to him.

"We don't allow dogs in the woods," Sal said. "I now know why."

Sal sat up. As he tried to stand, he let out a yelp. "My ankle."

"Lean on me," Olivia directed. Sal placed his hand on her shoulder. Each time he put weight on his ankle, he winced in pain. One step at a time, they made it to the front porch. Sweat ran down his face. "Stay," Olivia ordered, and pulled the rocking chair outside. Sal sat down with a sigh.

She knelt, untied his boot and pulled it off. The ankle had turned blue and swollen.

"What do I do?" Olivia raised eyes toward Sal. "Do you need a doctor?"

"I doubt that we could get to a doctor," Sal looked toward the bridge. "Find something to prop the foot on. Olivia ran to the house and returned with a dining room chair and pillow. She lifted the leg and rested the foot on the pillow. One look at his ashen face and Olivia ran back in the house. She came back with a glass of water and a wet cloth. Sal sipped the water and Olivia wiped his face and neck. Color crept back and Olivia breathed a sigh of relief.

"What can I do now?" Olivia asked.

"I have some whisky for medicinal purposes," Sal said. "You will find it in the cupboard by the sink. Olivia made her way to the kitchen and returned with the bottle and a glass. She handed the glass to Sal. He looked up at her. Tears streamed down her cheek. "Olivia?"

"Sorry." Olivia wiped at her eyes and poured Sal a small amount in the glass.

"Thanks," Sal said. "What's the matter?"

"My father drank." Olivia ran into the house. She washed her face and smoothed her hair. Composed once more, she came back to the porch.

"What about your mother?" Sal surprised her by asking.

"Mom left once." She wiped a stray tear from her eye. "She came back but things were never the same. She died not too long after that."

"You never talk about your father."

"What is there to talk about? He drank and after my mother

died, he kicked me out for being lazy."

"I'm sorry." Sal reached for her hand. He turned it over and planted a kiss in the palm. Olivia closed her fingers over the spot and drew it to her breast.

"Would you like something to eat?"

"Could you help me get inside?"

Olivia moved his foot off the pillow and pushed the chair out of the way. Sal held on to the wall as he maneuvered inside, dragging his foot. She rushed down the hall to turn back the quilt. With him ensconced in the bed, she set about making lunch. She checked in on him. His face looked pale against the quilt but he slept. Olivia backed out. Lunch could wait. He moaned in his sleep. At dusk, Olivia pulled the rocking chair beside the bed and settled in. Sleep overtook her.

****

"What time is it?" Sal asked.

"Good morning," Olivia leaned over and planted a kiss on his forehead. She moved the covers back and looked at the foot. The foot did not look as swollen. "Are you hungry?"

Sal reached for her hand. Olivia moved closer. "Time for that when you are back on your feet," she laughed from the door. "Breakfast will be ready shortly."

"Olivia," Sal pushed up to a sitting position, "the liquor is only used as a medicine around here." She studied his face for a moment. "I know."

She took sanctuary in the kitchen for a moment. Lady scratched at the door. Olivia opened the door and looked out. Lady ran to her feed pan. "Hungry?" She realized that she knew nothing about feeding. Composed now, she took Sal a plate. After he cleaned the plate, she asked about feeding the animals.

"I'll do it." Sal swung his feet to the floor. When he put weight on his foot, he winced in pain.

Olivia moved closer. "Sal, I can do it," she said. "You have to tell me what to do."

Sal nodded. "Help me make it to the porch and I tell you from there."

He leaned on her and hugged the wall. Together, they made it down the hall and out to the back porch. Lady came rushing up. She lay at Sal's feet as he told Olivia what to do and where to find the feed. She struggled but managed to get the job done.

She helped him back to bed where he fell asleep quickly. Olivia began to clean up and get lunch started.

"Olivia," Sal called. She ran down the hall.

"You OK?"

"I forgot the cow," Sal said. "Open the door and let her out. We can do without milk for a few days."

Olivia waded through the mud to the barn. She let the cow out and the calf came running. "Sorry about that," Olivia said as she pushed the calf over so she could get out. The hem of her dress caked in mud made walking difficult. Olivia pulled her shoes off at the door and stopped by the bathroom to shed her dress. She pulled the wrap around her and went to check on Sal.

He reached for her; she went to him. They made love in the middle of the afternoon with the sun pouring through the window. Sal moved Olivia on top. She felt in charge. She wondered if her mother ever had experienced such joy. Exhausted, they fell asleep. Olivia awoke to the room growing dark. She could feel his desire begin to rise and knew that he would be ready to go again. A sense of urgency washed over her. She had to get up. She felt her stomach growl and realized she had forgotten to eat. She would have to come clean with Sal soon.

Olivia and Sal repeated the routine each day. She helped him to the porch where he directed the feeding. By now, she could do it without Sal but she liked having him close. One day, Sal could stand on his ankle without wincing. Olivia knew he would be going back to work. The river crested and receded back into its banks. This morning, Sal pulled the truck around back to use it to pull the limbs out of the yard. He came back into the house to get the milk pail. Sal went toward the barn and Lady followed; she forgave Sal for tripping over her. Olivia smiled. She heard a vehicle stop at the front. Thinking it might be her egg customer, she headed to the front of the house. She did not recognize the truck at the gate but she knew the guy getting out on the passenger side. It was Tony.

Tony went to the door and knocked. Olivia came around the house.

"Can I help you?" Olivia said.

"I've come for Mom's things," Tony said.

"What things?" Olivia said, and moved to the porch.

"I don't have to explain to you," Tony raised his voice. He started to push past her when a hand grabbed his shoulder. Tony spun around.

"What are you doing?" Sal said.

"She wouldn't let me in," Tony stammered.

"It is her house," Sal said. He moved to stand by Olivia. "Go on inside." Sal opened the door for her.

"   I'll make coffee," she said. Olivia banged things in the kitchen so she could not hear the voices on the porch as they became louder.

"Olivia," Sal said and she jumped. "I didn't mean to startle you. Sit for a moment."

He took her hands and led her to the table. Sal took a chair. He looked deep in her eyes before he spoke. "Tony wants Mom's bed," Sal said. He looked drawn. Olivia reached up and rubbed her hand across his brow.

"What do you want?" Olivia said. She folded her hands and placed them on the table. Sal covered them with his big hand.

"We don't need it," Sal said.

"Fine," Olivia said. She pushed back her chair and brought Sal a mug of coffee.

He took the mug and went out the door. Tony and a man she did not know followed Sal down the hall and into the second bedroom. Sal returned to the table. They carried out the bed and then the dresser. Olivia raised an eyebrow.

"Marie wants it," Sal shrugged. He went out to the gate and closed it behind them.

Sal sat down in the chair he previously occupied. Olivia came up behind him and wrapped her arms around his neck. Sal pulled her onto his lap and held her close.

"I best get that cow milked," Sal said and headed out the back door. Olivia fixed the meal and they ate in silence. "I need to check the roof."

"Sal," Olivia said. She reached across the table for his hand.

"I'll be careful," he said.

Olivia held the ladder as Sal climbed up. He came to the top of the ladder and looked down. "Not much damage," he said. "Just a few shingles blown loose." Sal climbed back down the ladder and took it back to the shed.

She met him at the back door. She pounced, wrapped her legs around his waist and dug her nails into his back. His beard stubble scratched the soft inside of her arms and yet she held on. He swung her round and round until her hair came down from its customary tight chignon and wrapped about her shoulders.

His arms flew up around her with such fierceness that she could not breathe. He stunk of burnt oil; thrown off from wrestling the giant saw all day. She gave in to his strength. Her legs slid down the length of him until her toes touched the floor. She tangled her fingers in his hair and hung suspended there until her breathing became normal and their hearts began to beat in sync. Moisture welled in her eyes and rolled down onto the space above the top button of his shirt. He took a deep breath and released his grip just the slightest. His whisper in her ear was hardly more than a tickle. "Olivia, you are such a tiger." He grabbed her and spun her around until the white blur sucked them into a vortex where aching muscles and loneliness were forgotten in the closeness of the other. He sat on the couch holding her as if afraid she would disappear if he let go. Olivia laid her head on his shoulder and listened until their breathing slowed and their hearts beat as one.

****

Sal returned to work. Olivia insisted on helping him with the chores. She vowed she would learn to milk, no more not knowing how to do something. She moped around the house. She enjoyed having Sal around. "Better do something constructive," she chided herself. She made her way to the second bedroom. First, she scrubbed the floor and took the curtains down to wash them. With the furniture gone, she imagined how the room would look when she finished.

Olivia met Sal at the gate. He swung her up as though she weighed nothing. Olivia draped her arm around his neck. The smell of stew greeted them.

"That smells delicious."

"I hope it tastes as good as it smells." Olivia dished up the stew while Sal washed up. He cleared his bowl and started on a second. She grinned from ear to ear.

"This is good," Sal said between bites. "You are getting to be a great cook."

"Sal," Olivia said. "I thought I might clean the second bedroom. Your mother's things are still in there. What do you want done with them?" Olivia cleared the dishes off the table and stood with her back to Sal. He came up behind her and hugged her.

"Thanks," Sal said. "Guess I need to let Marie go through the things and see if there is anything she wants. Tony too, I guess." Sal nibbled on her ear.

"What about you?" Olivia said. "Is there anything you want?"

Sal paused for a moment. Olivia could feel the muscles in his arm tighten.

"Her comb," Sal said. "She had this decorative comb and brush set. I can see her sitting on the porch brushing her long hair, but I guess Marie wants it."

"You should have it," Olivia turned in his arms. "They have other things and that isn't asking for much. Keep the set for yourself."

Sal nodded and planted a kiss on the top of Olivia's head.

"Gather the things in a box and I'll drop it off at Marie's."

Saturday dawned clear. A gentle breeze swayed the trees and flowers. Olivia fixed breakfast and Sal fed the animals. He insisted that she take the day off from feeding. She sensed that he needed some time to himself. It took longer than usual for him to complete the chores. She cleaned up the kitchen and straightened the bed. She did not notice him standing in the doorway.

"You are beautiful," Sal said. "How did I get so lucky?" Color crept up Olivia's neck and bathed her face in a warm glow.

"I am the lucky one." She hung the dishrag over the sink. "Why did you marry me?"

"You were so darn independent. You looked like a drowned rat but you didn't take handouts," Sal smiled, remembering the day they met. Unlike his family, she never took things for granted and she pulled her own weight. Sal knew how lucky he had been that the wind blew Olivia into his life. He couldn't imagine anything more that he could need.

"I could ask the same thing. Why did you marry me?" Sal crossed his arms.

"Before you came along, I found no reason to get out of bed," Olivia said. "Life seemed empty and cold. You saved me."

"We saved each other." Sal pushed off the wall.

"Are you ready to go?"

"Go?" Sal nodded.

Olivia nodded. She did not ask where they were going, for she feared the answer.

Sal closed the truck door and went around. Olivia settled back and enjoyed the view. Everything glowed green. The trees leafed out and the flowers popped up beside the road. She hummed the song Sal sang at church. She'd developed a habit of doing so.

As they neared town, she hushed, clinched her hands in her lap and shot sidelong glances at Sal. He stared straight ahead. At a fork in the road, he turned the truck away from town. She looked at him. He reached out and took her hand in his.

She did not ask where they were going but it was evident that town lay in the opposite direction. It had been a long time since Olivia had come down this road, catching a ride with the mail truck. She tightened her grip on Sal's hand. When he stopped at the cemetery, Olivia sat frozen in place. "Wait here." He began walking up and down between the stones, searching for something.

Sal came back and opened the door. Olivia slid out and stood in front of him.

He took her hand and led her toward the gate. She had not been here since her mother's funeral. Sal stopped in front of a grave and Olivia read the name. *McKay*.

"My father?" She stooped down and ran her fingers over the writing. The date indicated that her father had died not long after he kicked her out.

"He can't hurt you anymore," Sal said.

Olivia let the tears fall. He patted her on the shoulder, and then walked a few steps away. The sun peaked out from behind the clouds and bathed her in a warm glow. Peace flowed through her and tears no longer did as Olivia rejoined Sal. She took his hand and led him to her mother's grave.

"Mom," Olivia said. "This is Sal. You would like him. He is kind and takes such great care of me. He's going to make a wonderful father." Sal slipped his arm around Olivia's waist. She moved his arm down to her stomach and whispered the one word she had tried to tell him, "Baby."

Sal could not speak. He held Olivia tighter. Joy shone from his eyes like a beacon, and finally from his lips the words came, "I love you."

How could she have doubted him? Then she understood. It wasn't him she had doubted, but her own worth. He spun her around again and then sat her down gently. "I didn't hurt you, did I?" Olivia shook her head.

"A baby, we are going to have a baby!"

"I am glad you brought me here today," Olivia said. "I thought we were going to see Marie and Tony."

"From now on, we start our own traditions," Sal said. "We will change Mom's room into a nursery. She would be so excited. Do you feel OK?"

"OK? I feel great." She put the past to rest there in the graveyard. From now on, her family consisted of Sal and the baby. No bad dreams, no seeing her father lurking about. She was happy. "Sal, let's stop by and tell your family and invite them over for lunch tomorrow."

Sal stood with his mouth open. "You mean it?" He grabbed Olivia and spun her around again. "Why?"

"They are your family," she said.

The two made their way back to the truck. Sal closed the door, leaned through the window and kissed Olivia. "I have never been so happy. A baby…we are going to have a baby and that will make me a Daddy." Olivia smiled.